To Scratch a Witch

A WATER WITCH MYSTERY
BOOK TWO

LEAH R CUTTER

KNOTTED ROAD PRESS

Reviews
It's true. Reviews help me sell more books. If you've enjoyed this story, please consider leaving a review of it on your favorite site.

Come someplace new...
Are you a traveler? Do you enjoy exploring strange new worlds, new cultures, new people?

Sign up for my newsletter and I'll start you on your travels with a free copy of my book, *The Island Sampler*.

http://www.LeahCutter.com/newsletter/

Buy More!
Did you know that you can buy directly from the Knotted Road Press website?

https://www.knottedroadpress.com/shop/

The Guardian Hound

War Among the Crocodiles

The Cassie Stories

Poisoned Pearls

Tainted Waters

Spoiled Harvest

Bloodied Ice

Epic Fantasy Series

The Fallen Elves

Ruins of the Gods

Stairs of the Gods

Cities of the Gods

Graves of the Gods

Houses of the Dead

Houses Divided

Houses Fallen

Houses Reborn

Forgotten Gods

A Wind Blown Torment

A Stone Strewn Clash

A Sea Washed Victory

The Tanesh Empire Trilogy

The Glass Magician

The Desert Heart

The Ghost Dog

Science Fiction

The Long Run

Project Nemesis

Project Nyx

Project Tisiphone

Project Persephone

War of the Allied Worlds

The Labors of Darius Linard

Huli Intergalactic: Science/Space Fantasy

Origins

The Strawberry Girl

Chapter One

"ARE WE THERE YET?" AJ teased her sister Bea as they reached Highway 101 heading north.

Bea glared at AJ. "Don't you make me turn this car around," she warned in mock seriousness.

AJ snorted. Honestly, having Bea drive her around so she could play at being the bratty little sister had been *so* much fun this summer. Generally, AJ had to be the responsible, practical older sister while her younger sister was the artistic blonde airhead.

"Remind me why I'm even taking you here?" Bea said as she merged with traffic.

There weren't that many cars on the highway, despite the fact that it was the end of September and the weather on the Washington State coast was kind of nice. All right, there were enough gray clouds to ruin any picnic, the wind was sharp, and the heavens were certain to dump more rain on them anytime now.

But it wasn't currently raining. The trees had held onto their fall glory so far which mean the scenery was beautiful.

And AJ hadn't bothered to buy a new car (or at least new to her), which meant that until Bea went back to Seattle, her younger sister was her chauffeur.

"We're going to the county historical society," AJ said, "which is located in Sunset, the next big town up the coast from Milltown. It's got weird hours, which is why we're going up on a Wednesday afternoon. And we're going so that I can see if I can find more information about Gladys, the ghost haunting the Bridgewater Inn, as well as her death."

Bea shook her head. "Six months ago, if you'd told me that my business-minded, stupidly successful big sister believed in ghosts enough to go do *research* on them, I'd have assumed you were having one on me. Or high. Or both."

AJ merely shrugged. A lot had happened in those intervening six months, since she'd left Seattle and moved down to Milltown that spring, in May.

Originally, it wasn't supposed to be a permanent move. AJ had just come down for the summer, to stay with Bea at her cottage while getting her life back together again and figuring out what her next move was.

However, AJ had found work managing the Bridgewater Inn, work that made her happy while not running her completely ragged.

She'd also discovered her true calling as a water witch, gifted with visions of the future, as well as the ability to work with water in various magical ways.

"Why can't Gladys just tell you about herself?" Bea asked, still clearly put out by the entire trip. She was giving up an afternoon painting. She, too, was stupidly successful, as an artist, though, her boogie boho paintings hitting the cultural zeitgeist at just the right time.

AJ couldn't help but sigh. "I don't think she's completely clear on the concept. If I ask who she is, all she repeats is that she's Gladys. She ignores me when I ask for a middle or last name. When I asked if she was Oscar Byrne's daughter or wife, all she said was, 'Yes.' When I tried to question her further, she disappeared for two days."

"You don't suppose she's an amalgamation of both the dead daughter and wife?" Bea said.

"I have no idea if that's even possible," AJ said. "Ursula doesn't have much experience with ghosts, so she can't tell me either." Ursula was also a water witch, and was AJ's mentor. However, their powers were different, so much of the time AJ had to figure things out on her own. Though Ursula now lived across the country with her sister, they still regularly talked on the phone.

"Speaking of Ursula, how's the construction going?" Bea asked.

When Ursula had moved away from Milltown to go live with her sister in Georgia, she'd sold AJ the beautiful Craftsman house right on the beach. The price had been right, particularly given the amount of work the house had needed.

"Didn't I tell you? The final inspection was on Monday. The foundation passed," AJ said.

"What a relief!" Bea exclaimed.

"It really was. You have no idea how scared I've been that there was going to be yet *another* delay," AJ admitted. "And the exterior paint job is finished so I no longer live in what looks like a children's ice cream parlor."

Bea snorted at that. "Yeah, that color scheme was never going to fly with you. I'm glad you listened to me, though, and didn't go all somber."

AJ couldn't help but roll her eyes. "The dark-gray walls and maroon trim would have looked sophisticated. The color scheme you originally came up with was just as bad, if not worse, than the original candy land. Orange and red?" She didn't bother to hide her shudder.

"As I explained, those are sunset colors. Perfect for a beach house facing the Pacific Ocean. I can't help it that you have no sense of taste," Bea said. "But I am happy with what you eventually chose."

"Me too," AJ said. The original house had been painted white, pink, and teal. AJ had found a company to repaint it a softer white, almost cream color, that in certain lights looked like a reflection of the sand. The trim she'd finally ended up with was a burnt sienna, which held onto Bea's concept of sunset while still appealing to AJ's admittedly more somber tastes.

Only one portion of the roof shingles bothered her still, the witch's hat that was on top of the round tower that stood just to the right of the front door. However, with the new color scheme, it no longer looked so pink. The rest of the roof was a very sensible light gray, and wouldn't need replacing for a few years.

Which was good, because AJ was already spending *so much money* repairing and renovating the rest of the house.

"When are you opening up for psychic consults?" Bea asked, aiming for innocence but missing by at least a mile. She'd been bugging AJ about it all summer.

"You know that Ursula asks that every time we talk, right?" AJ said, aggrieved.

"It was part of the agreement for her selling the house to you," Bea said.

"Which, as we both know, was totally not legal or enforceable," AJ said, possibly a little too heatedly.

She made herself take a deep breath. Since entering into perimenopause earlier that year, her emotions were far too close to the surface now. Just about anything would set her off.

"So when are you going to do it?" Bea asked, determinedly.

"This weekend," AJ admitted. "It's the first weekend in October. I'm doing it as part of that whole 'witch-tober' thing that half the businesses in town are going in on."

Bea grinned. "Really? You're going to start doing readings and such? This Saturday?"

AJ rolled her eyes. "Yes. I'm not ready though. Ursula has had me practicing with the tarot cards, memorizing all the possible divination meanings for each card, both upright as well as reversed. She's even tested me on it," AJ groused.

"Don't give me that," Bea scolded. "You love tests. You've always excelled at tests."

"Yeah, well, this...this is different," AJ stuttered.

"How? How is this different?" Bea counted. "It's a bunch of facts for you to memorize. How is that different?"

"They don't make any sense," AJ whined. She hated that she was whining, and yet she continued to do so. "The queen of swords, with her hand raised, represents sterility.

And yet, there are butterflies carved into her throne. She should represent chrysalis. Death, yes, but rebirth as well."

When Bea didn't say anything, AJ finally looked over at her. Her sister was pressing her full lips together tightly and there was mischief dancing in her blue eyes.

"What," AJ said flatly, not sure she wanted to hear.

"Sounds like you *are* ready," Bea said. "Just following your own path, because you couldn't possibly be conventional and follow the same road that everyone else goes down, now, could you? Even when it comes to the occult?"

AJ opened her mouth, then closed it again. "I'm not saying you're right," she said slowly as the realization took hold. "But you might not be wrong either."

Bea snorted at her. "And everyone says that *I'm* the flighty, artistic one. You're just as bad. You've never allowed it to show before."

"I'm not sure I'd go that far," AJ said. Some of the psychic work, as well as her magical abilities, made her deeply uncomfortable. They were so outside the norm that she'd worked so hard to maintain her entire life.

Particularly the water magic. Ursula had a lovely fountain in her backyard. Between the high fence and the location, no one could see in. AJ had spent some of her time that summer working with the water, getting it to form a large arc and land ten feet away with the smallest of gestures on her part. She'd also developed something of a water shield as well. It wouldn't stop a bullet, but it might protect her from a thrown punch.

She always felt guilty afterward, though, as if she'd been doing something dirty, not just abnormal.

"I get it," Bea said softly. "It's hard to change. Particularly when you're going through *the* change."

AJ grunted at that. "Stupid body. Can't decide if my periods are over or not. One minute I'm fine. Then I have cramps. Nothing happens, just cramps. Then I'm fine again. That by itself is enough to drive anyone crazy. Then you add in the night sweats and occasional hot flash."

"Can't wait," Bea sarcastically replied.

"Mom assured me that it wouldn't last too long, though," AJ said. "Maybe a year." She'd started perimenopause a little early at forty-two, according to her doctor, but right on time, according to her mother, who said that her grandmothers on both sides of the family had started early as well.

"Mmm," Bea said, just nodding.

The sisters drove along in silence for a little while.

"Are we there yet?"

Chapter Two

THE BYRNE COUNTY Historical Society building was just off the main drag of Sunset, in a 1950s wood-shingled structure, painted a somber brown that didn't add anything to its curb-appeal. The front of the it rose up into a steep peak with windows set at the top, while the rest of the roof was perpendicular to it with a more modest pitch. It gave off a whole churchy vibe. However, based on the porch that ran across the front as well as the sides, AJ would bet that it had originally been someone's home.

A chimney rose up on the right side of the building, sticking up like the front steepled portion of the roof, another impediment her eye caught on instead of allowing it to slide across. A modern metal baffle covered the top of it so that someone could have a fire and not have gale-force winds flowing down into the room below. Roses bushes lined the edges of the tiny yard, the leaves brown and falling. AJ would bet that come summer when they bloomed, the scent was divine. An old apple tree took up one corner, lichen clinging to its sprawling branches, giving it a misshapen, spooky look.

If AJ hadn't known that this was the site of the historical society, she might have delicately inquired whether the owner was, in fact, a witch or some other weird denizen.

"Cozy," Bea said, sarcasm dripping, as she walked up the cracking sidewalk.

"It's probably maintained with volunteer work." AJ said, unsure why she felt as though she had to defend it. The winds were quiet for now, but AJ was still glad she wore her heavier rain jacket, a T-shirt and sweater underneath, as well as jeans and boots. She'd been slowly adding to her "non-work" wardrobe all summer, so while her choices were few, she really liked everything she had in her closet.

The squeak the solid wood door gave as AJ pushed it in was impressive. Not quite enough to wake the dead, but surely as good as any bell hanging over the lintel, warning that visitors had entered.

Inside, the impression of a former private house continued, given how the space was divided and rooms set off the main entranceway.

Somber wood paneling covered the walls. Chestnut-colored wooden planks made up the floor. The canned ceiling lights barely raised the setting to *dim*. To the left stood a long desk, also made out of wood and roughly assembled, with the "reception" sign done as little logs on a plate.

For all the wood in the place, it smelled much more of old books and dusty cushions, the air a bit chilly.

Roland came out from a curtained door behind the desk. "Hi, AJ! Bea! Good to see you!"

AJ smiled at Roland, glad that he was the one they'd be dealing with that day. He was the unofficial historian for Milltown, and gave ghost tours of the buildings on Main Street all summer. The last tour would be in about a month's time, on the weekend before Halloween (which fell awkwardly on a Wednesday that year).

He didn't look like her idea of a historian, with his full dark beard, meaty hands, and lumberjack black-and-red-checked flannel shirt. He didn't even wear glasses. She kept expecting to see him carrying a beer can. His nails were bitten to the quick, but at least they didn't have dirt embedded underneath them. He was about her age, in his mid-forties.

"Good to see you too, Roland," AJ said as she walked up to the counter. "How are you?"

"Can't complain," Roland said. He seemed to give the question some actual thought. "Yep. Can't complain, not really. How are you two doing?"

"Good," Bea said. "Even though I did have to drive up here with someone constantly asking if we were there yet." She gave AJ a mock glare.

"What? Getting you back for all your years as a bratty younger sister has made today an *excellent* day," AJ said, unrepentant.

Roland merely grinned as he glanced from one sister to the other. "So what can I help you with today? What are you looking to research?" Then he paused and looked at AJ. "Oooh, are you looking for more of the history of the inn?"

AJ tilted her head from side to side. "Sort of." She took a breath, wondering how much she should tell him.

Milltown was a *small* town. Though the population was around sixteen thousand, everyone knew everyone else's business. It was something she was still getting used to.

At some point, particularly after she opened up her "shop" as a psychic, people were going to learn more about her powers.

Still, she hesitated. Roland waited patiently. After a few moments, AJ said, "I'm actually looking for information about the first owners. Oscar Byrne, and his wife, Gladys."

"And?" Bea prompted AJ.

"Fine," AJ said with huff. "And more about Gladys, the ghost who haunts the inn."

Roland did run the ghost tours for the buildings on Main Street, right? Surely he knew about ghosts and such. Maybe even believed in them. He wouldn't give her a hard time about that. Hopefully.

"Gladys is a tough one," Roland admitted, running one hand through his hair and adorably mussing it. "The papers of the time didn't bother reporting about women, not unless they were doing something exotic, like going after their husbands with an ax."

"Did that happen much? In Byrne county?" AJ had to ask.

"Just once," Roland said with a grin. "If you come on my ghost tour this weekend, you'll hear all about it."

AJ shook her head. "Kind of busy this weekend," she said. And she was. She was officially going to "open" as a psychic. She didn't think she'd have too many people pounding on her door, but she wasn't about to close early just to go on Roland's tour.

She'd paid for an ad for her new business—Ocean Waves Psychic Readings—in the local newspaper, which would be available tomorrow morning, offering a free, fifteen minute consult. She was running the special both Friday and Saturday evenings, as suggested by Ursula. AJ had been doing rapid readings every day to practice, just a three-card draw from the tarot deck, past, present, and future. It was hard, though, with only herself and no one to work with. She was kind of looking forward to having a bunch of guinea pigs to practice on.

While she'd known that Bea would have been happy to help, AJ also wasn't thrilled with the idea of knowing too much about her sister. There were just some things that an older sister shouldn't be privy to. Ranked right up there with any details about her mom and dad, though the couple was long divorced.

"You'll have to come on the ghost tour some other time, then," Roland said.

"I'd like that," AJ said, a bit curious. This felt suspiciously as though Roland was kinda sorta asking her out on a date, albeit with a ton of other people coming along.

"What can you tell us about Gladys?" Bea asked.

"Her sightings started with the first guests to the inn, back in 1913," Roland said.

"Wait, I thought the inn was built in 1912?" AJ said.

"Ground was broken and the foundation was laid in 1912," Roland said, nodding. "But the inn itself didn't open for business until 1913. And even then, it was touch-

and-go for a while. There were some issues with the financing, but those got smoothed over that spring."

"So who were the first guests? Who saw Gladys?" AJ asked.

"The story is mentioned in a book of ghost stories collected from the area," Roland said. "I believe it was published back in 1925. Not a formal book, more like a pamphlet."

"Do you have it here? Can I see it?" AJ asked.

"We do!" Roland said. "We have a copy of it that you can look at, as we are trying to preserve the original."

Roland came out from behind the counter and led AJ and Bea over to the room on the other side of the front entranceway. "This is the reading room," Roland said.

The room went all the way from the front of the house to the back. AJ would bet that it had been chopped up into more than one room when originally built, but opened up later into a much nicer setting. The front looked like a coffee shop, with scruffy, obviously second-hand couches and chairs around the huge fireplace. Three tables stood in the back half of the room, with mismatched wooden chairs around them.

Roland brought them water in glasses—more Goodwill chic—that had "sippy cup" tops on them, so they wouldn't spill accidentally on any of their reading material.

"Are there gloves we're supposed to wear?" AJ asked as she sat down.

"Naw, they discovered that wearing gloves was actually more harmful to the books than human fingers," Roland told them. Then he went upstairs to where most of the books were located. While there were public stacks down here on the first floor, the more valuable books were kept upstairs in a locked room.

As AJ went through the pamphlet Roland brought her, she saw that he'd been correct, there wasn't much to the story of Gladys's first sighting. A banker and his wife had spent a night at the inn in July 1913, about a month after its grand opening in June of that year. The woman (who didn't rate a name, of course) said that she'd heard a noise out in the hallway, like a young woman weeping.

When she'd opened the door, a cold wind blew by her. Then her husband woke up and said that the ghost had walked through the door, past the foot of the bed, and out through the wall.

"Hmmm," AJ said after reading the account and showing it to Bea. "Doesn't mention what room they were staying in."

"Probably one of the ones on the first floor," Roland said.

"Why would you think that?" AJ asked.

He shrugged. "The vast majority of her sightings are on the first floor," he said. "There's been less than a handful on the other floors."

AJ realized that she'd only seen Gladys on the first floor. Then again, that was where the office was, the one that AJ worked out of. She herself rarely went upstairs.

"This account doesn't give her a name," AJ said. "When did someone first refer to her as Gladys?"

"There are a couple in the 1930s," Roland said. "But I've always wondered if that's her real name."

"She said she was Gladys, when I asked her," AJ said.

It took her a moment to realize that Roland was staring hard at her.

Damn it! She hadn't meant to tell anyone that she could talk with the ghost. Though that communication wasn't consistent. Gladys appeared to take time to build up strength, and so only spoke a little with AJ before she fizzled out. Some days were definitely better than others.

"You asked her?" Roland said after a few moments.

AJ sighed and looked at Bea for support.

Her bratty little sister just smirked at her and sat back, crossing her arms over her chest, a clear indication that AJ was on her own with this.

"Uhm, the reason why I'm busy this weekend and can't go on your tour is because I'm reopening the psychic busi-ness, in Ursula's old house," AJ admitted. That was at least telling him something without giving away the entire farm, right?

"Really?" Roland said, obviously surprised. "That's so cool! Do you have business cards? I'd be happy to have them on hand for the ghost tours."

"I do, actually, but not with me," AJ said. "Or not that many." She hadn't thought to pair up with Roland's tours, but it was perfect synergy, a term that she'd quickly learned to hate when it came to software development. However, here, it actually applied.

"Did Gladys come to you in a reading or something?" Roland said, still obviously curious about the ghost.

"Something," AJ said.

"I know that when Eva and Irv ran the place, she was always knocking down the pictures on the walls of their office," he said. "And the one time they'd tried having an open kiosk with postcards out in the lobby, she'd made a mess of everything."

"Eva told me about that," AJ said. "Why would you think Gladys wasn't her name?"

Roland shrugged. "Just seemed too convenient, you know? Both Mrs. Byrne as well as her daughter were named Gladys. Then there's a ghost named Gladys. It was a popular name. She might be related to the Byrnes. She might not be."

AJ sighed and nodded. "I do think her name is Gladys. But I don't know who she is. I was hoping you might have some records that would help."

Roland shook his head. "I'd like to tell you that of course, we know everything that happened in the past. We're the historical society, after all." He gave her a knowing smirk. "But Gladys really is a mystery. There are a couple of books that mention her and give longer accounts, but I don't know if any of the stories in them are real."

AJ sighed, disappointed. She'd really thought that if anyone knew about Gladys, it would be the people here.

"Sure, I'd love to see some other reports of the ghost," she said after a few moments, trying not to sound ungrateful. "That would be great."

Roland nodded and headed back upstairs to get them some books. As soon as he left, Bea leaned over the table.

"He's kinda cute," she said.

AJ looked at her, perplexed. "Maybe? If you're into that whole manly-man thing."

Bea snorted at her. "Right. Because a guy who can chop his own firewood as well as quote Shakespeare at you isn't sexy at all."

AJ just shrugged. She'd always gone for the pure braini-acs, not the poets.

And look how well that had worked for her. Her ex, Ken, had cheated on her in her own damned house. AJ wasn't certain she was ready for a new relationship. It had only been six months and she was still, quite frankly, pissed off about the whole thing.

Still, when Roland deposited the books on the table, she did take a moment to really look at him.

She had to admit that the full beard was more hipster than woodsman given that it was well trimmed and his neck was shaven. His eyes were a solid warm brown and full of intelligence, and his eyebrows weren't wild bits of fur but also had been tamed. Flecks of gray were just starting to appear at his temples, and she knew that he'd grow more ruggedly handsome as the years went on. Broad shoulders filled out his flannel shirt, the kind that came from honest work and not from the gym. His hands were beefy, weathered, and scarred, like an old woodsman. However, he smelled nice, a subtle woodsy smell, not some obnoxious chemical scent that other guys sprayed on by the gallon.

He gave her a smile as he handed out the books, and was about to go into more depth about his choices when the door gave its characteristic groan as someone else entered.

"Yoo hoo, Roland!" came a woman's voice.

Roland's posture tightened suddenly, as if preparing for battle. "If you ladies will excuse me?" he said, already rising and going toward the door.

"Yes, Mrs. Reed?" Roland said. He sounded angry, as well as resigned.

"Please, dear, call me Phoebe," the woman insisted. "I have another box of books for you to go through!"

"Determining the value of rare books isn't my forte," Roland insisted.

"But there are a few books about supernatural sightings," Phoebe countered. "They're out in the car. Let's go fetch them together, shall we?"

"Yes, Mrs. Reed," Roland said.

Their voices faded as they walked away, out the door.

AJ looked up at Bea, who had a curious look on her face. "That's Phoebe Reed. She runs one of bookstores in Milltown. Reed's Reads."

"I don't think I know her," AJ said. She didn't recall meeting the woman at any of the chamber of commerce meetings that she'd attended so far.

Bea shrugged. "She isn't that active in town. Considers herself too successful for the rest of us peons." She gave AJ a smirk. "She sure seems interested in Roland. You'll have to make your play soon."

AJ rolled her eyes. "Please. I get the impression that Roland isn't that interested in her, that it's all one-sided."

"You may be right," Bea said.

The sisters returned to their respective books, listening to Phoebe and Roland go in and out of the door to the historic society building a few times.

AJ found the next account of Gladys fanciful in the extreme. Had Gladys ever actually been found weeping and wringing her hands as she walked down one of the hallways? AJ doubted it. The ghost wouldn't waste her energy that way. Though she did vaguely recall Eva spreading that tale.

AJ tried to focus on the words in front of her, but something was bothering her. It was almost as if Gladys was there in the room with them, trying to get AJ's attention.

Finally, she glanced up.

No, a ghost hadn't joined them there.

However, the water in her glass had started to glow.

Damn it!

She was about to have another vision.

And this one felt like a doozy.

What could she do? She didn't want to have a vision, not here in a public space. But she wasn't sure she could hold this one off. It felt like a hot flash, suddenly drenching all of her senses. Her legs had gone numb. If she tried to stand, she'd be unable to hold up her weight.

AJ hissed at Bea, then pointed to her glass of water.

Could her sister see any of the weirdness happening there?

Bea looked annoyed at the interruption. "What?" she mouthed silently.

AJ didn't speak. Couldn't. Couldn't even keep her gaze on Bea, but found her eyes irrevocably drawn back to the glass of water.

"Ohhh," she finally heard Bea breathe out. "Nope. Don't see anything," her sister continued in a whisper.

AJ nodded. "Guard…" she finally managed to say.

Fortunately, Bea appeared to understand what AJ meant. She got up out of her chair and took a stance in the archway that was at the entrance of the room, preventing anyone from coming closer and disturbing AJ.

With trembling hands, AJ pulled the glass toward her, pushing the books to the side, out of the way.

The top covering the glass practically flew off when AJ applied her thumbs to it, emitting a loud *pop* and somersaulting away, as if the glass had become pressurized.

Thick fog covered the water. AJ brought her overly warm hands up to hold the cool glass. It felt like it contained ice water, though she knew the water hadn't been that cold, not when Roland had served it to her.

The fog cleared away quickly, leaving the top of the water silvery-gray, like a mirror.

An image slowly rose from the depth, pushing up through the surface of the water. At first, it looked like a puff of white smoke, at least until AJ figured out that she was looking at the back of a full head of white hair.

She couldn't help but shiver as the head rotated and she caught a glimpse of the face on the other side.

It was an older woman, her lips shaped in a perpetual frown. She wore too much makeup, unsuccessfully trying to hide her wrinkles. Her nose was sharp, just the type to get into other people's business. Her eyes were closed.

AJ knew that she'd never open them again.

More of her face became visible as the vision rose up. Something had been wrapped around her neck. It wasn't rope. It looked more like a string of numbers that had artfully choked her to death.

"AJ?"

AJ started at the sound of her name. Lukewarm water from the cup splashed over her hands, the vision broken.

Which was good, because she wasn't sure she wanted to see more.

"Are you okay?" Roland asked as he came into the room.

"Yes, fine," AJ said, scrambling to cover her weirdness. "I accidentally spilled my water, after you'd told us not to."

"I got it," Roland said, hurrying over to pick up a roll of paper towels sitting on a corner of the table and tearing her off a few sheets. "That's why we had the lids on them."

AJ didn't blush. Not really. All she felt was a little heat in her cheeks.

She'd tried for so long to be "normal." To be her mother's successful daughter, working as a manager, making her first fortune when the little startup she'd been a part of had been bought.

To be caught doing something as weird as having a vision was still deeply unsettling to her. As well as not obeying the rules, by taking the lid off her glass.

She glanced at Bea, who was still standing at the edge of the archway, talking with a woman who'd stayed there, away from the table.

An older woman. With great clouds of white hair. Her mouth slanted down into a frown.

AJ stiffened with shock, though she managed to contain her gasp.

Phoebe Reed, she'd bet. Of Reed's Reads.

The woman she'd seen dead in her glass.

And given the way that Roland glared at her over his shoulder when she called his name, AJ was possibly in the same room as her killer.

Chapter Three

AJ WAITED until she and Bea were in the car, heading back to Milltown, before she gave in to her sister's questions and told her everything about the vision.

"Phoebe Reed? Really?" Bea exclaimed. "And you think Roland might kill her?"

"I don't know," AJ said. "Really, I don't. He just was looking awfully murderous at her, you know?"

"How do we stop her from being killed?" Bea said.

"I don't think we can," AJ said, feeling helpless. "I saw her already dead. It wasn't symbolic. It was her face."

"What about those numbers around her neck? Those weren't real, right?" Bea said. "Maybe we can stop those from getting close to her."

AJ shook her head. "Maybe. I just don't think so. I think she's a dead lady walking."

Bea shivered at that, and they both sat in the car silent for a few moments, uncomfortable truths wrapping icy fingers across their shoulders.

"Phoebe Reed owns a bookstore," Bea finally countered. "She isn't an accountant. Why would she be killed by numbers?"

"I don't know," AJ said, frustrated. She felt as though the numbers around Phoebe Reed's neck were a clue. She just didn't know what it meant.

"Tell me what you know about Roland," AJ said. "What's his story?"

Bea thought for a moment before replying. "He's a local. Both his parents are lawyers. They live in the southern part of Milltown, where the real money still is. Roland went to Whitman for college, then was supposed to go to Gonzaga, I think. Was supposed to go into law. Had fallen in love with history, though. Got a PhD in it, then couldn't find a teaching job. Came back here and has been running his own lawn and gardening business ever since."

"Huh," AJ said. She could tell he worked with his hands. "Successful, I'm assuming?"

Bea shrugged. "More or less. He has his own place and isn't dependent on his parents, if that's what you're asking. Drives a beater, though, doesn't own a mansion or beach-front property. He does well enough."

"Do you think he would kill Phoebe Reed?" AJ said. "For her being so annoying, if nothing else?"

"I don't think so," Bea said. She gave AJ a tight smile. "He's a history professor, under all that lumberjack exterior. I don't think he's secretly a murderer."

AJ tilted her head from side to side. She didn't know. She didn't know either of them well enough.

And she suspected she didn't have time to get to know Phoebe.

"When we get back, can we stop at her bookstore?" AJ asked. "Just to look around?"

"You're not afraid of walking in on a dead body?" Bea asked, surprised.

AJ grimaced. "There is that," she said. "But we left before she did, so I doubt she'll get there before we do. I'd like to see the place. Before she dies. Maybe there's some way we could save her."

Bea snorted. "I admire the way you say, 'we.' As if you think I'm the one with any ideas here." She drummed her fingers across the steering wheel. "I'm leaving on Monday. Five days from now. You're going to have to figure this out quickly if you want any input from me."

AJ opened her mouth, then shut it again.

No, her bratty little sister was right.

Unless this all got wrapped up this weekend, she was going to be on her own solving a crime that hadn't even occurred yet.

They sat in silence the rest of the short ride back to Milltown, the rain spattering the car a couple of times as they drove in and out of squall lines. Leaves swirled up on the sides of the road as scattered winds blew. Fall was AJ's second favorite season, with spring being the first, and she tried to enjoy the colors as they sped down the highway.

For all her heavy thoughts, AJ couldn't help but smile as they crested the last hill and the ocean opened up on the horizon, a dark gray line full of opportunity.

She was never going to get used to that sight. Hell, the view from her house was pretty sweet as well, as she now lived on the beach and got to listen to the waves every night when she went to sleep. She was looking forward to seeing what the ocean was like across all the seasons.

They wound down the steep incline heading to the town. They drove all the way down to Main Street before turning left and driving along the main drag, going to the bookshop.

As Bea had once said, Milltown was two miles long and two blocks wide, or at least the commercial district was. There were plenty of homes and vacation rentals stretched out among the hills overlooking the town. While Bea lived on the northern edge in a more modest neighborhood, the southern end of town, closer to the old sawmills which had given the town its name, was much richer, with mansions tucked in amongst the pines.

AJ enjoyed the drive down the street, admiring the buildings. Milltown had severely suffered the economic downturn of the 1970s, and it hadn't been developed at that time, when so many other places had been. This meant that a lot of the original buildings from the 1900s still graced the area, only being revitalized in the last twenty years.

Due to people like Roland, many of the properties had been placed on the historic registry, including AJ's house. There were rules she had to follow in terms of renovating the place. However, it also meant that it couldn't be razed to the ground and ugly condos put up instead, something she'd seen happen again and again in her old neighborhood in Seattle.

Reed's Reads turned out to be in one of the more modern buildings, probably constructed in the 1950s, close to the southern-most public beach access. The single-story building was done in stucco, painted a soft orangish-pink, while dark red tiles covered the roof. Huge signs in the parking lot warned of *No Walk Offs, Yes, That Means You.*

AJ understood that could be a problem, particularly this close to the beach access. Tourists would park their cars in the bookstore parking lot and then go to the beach, leaving no place for customers. The city tried to address this and provide adequate parking closer to the beach. However, the number of tourists had swelled considerably, and the population of sixteen thousand could triple on a holiday weekend.

The bookstore windows had all been painted over from the inside, or filled with signs, such as the one next to the dark red door, "Get your summer beach reads here!" It looked cute enough on the outside, the walls and the roof in good repair.

However, AJ immediately felt claustrophobic stepping inside. Bookcases stuffed with books lined the small entranceway. The smell of mold tickled the back of her throat. How long before her eyes started watering? At least the floor was made up from Spanish tiles, that same dark red as the roof, with charcoal gray grouting. Probably to hide the dirt better.

Just past the small hallway to the left stood a desk with a register and a sullen young man sitting behind it. He didn't bother to look up from his phone to greet his customers.

Bookcases marched across the floor, with narrow aisles between them. They blocked the light and made the room feel tight and pinched. Books had been haphazardly crammed into the shelves, some vertical, some horizontal.

More books were heaped in piles on the floor beside the bookcases, making excellent fire hazards. In fact, some of the bookcases themselves appeared to be made out of towering stacks of books and would probably fall over in a stiff wind. Faded yellow tags taped to the shelves categorized each section. However, they were badly out of date as more books had come in and been shoved into place.

This wasn't a place where books were treated lovingly. Nor was it a place that knew much about soap and dusters.

All of it offended AJ's sense of order. She hadn't been that much of a reader for most of her adult life as she'd been too busy with her job. She'd work ten to twelve hours a day, heat food up in the microwave, watch an hour of something brainless on the TV, then drag herself off to bed, only to do it again the next day.

Since being down in Milltown, she'd started reading again, though primarily ebooks. She couldn't stand anything that had even the slightest hint of paranormal in it. She had enough of that in her real life, thank-you-very-much. Instead, she found herself drawn to murder mysteries and true crime. She'd tried medical thrillers, but in the last one she'd picked up the main character had gone from "nosy busybody" to "too stupid to live" in a hurry. Thrillers left her cold—were there really that many world-wide conspiracies being hatched?

Still, she went to the back of the shop to browse what appeared to be the mystery/thriller section, while Bea stayed out front to look at the art books (of course).

The books AJ found were all older. She doubted that anything on the shelves had been published in the twenty-first century. Many of the books were in disrepair, the covers torn or the pages swollen with water damage. More than one had sections underlined and pages folded down to mark a previous owner's favorite passages.

The smell of mold was stronger back here between the stacks. AJ was going to need a shower when they left, to get rid of it. She left her area and went to find Bea in short order. This wasn't a comfortable place for browsing, not unless one was intent on digging through piles of dreck for a questionable diamond.

Bea was looking through shelves that were unfortunately located underneath one of the painted-over windows, making it difficult to see the books. Bea had to tilt her head to the side so that she could read the titles. Her mouth was pressed together tightly in disappointment and she kept shaking her head.

"Find anything?" AJ asked as she came up.

"Nothing," Bea said, sounding disgusted. "Nothing interesting. No books on theory, just pictograms of other artists. Coffee table books."

"You know art theory?" AJ teased. Bea's works tended to be more abstract than realistic.

Bea just rolled her eyes. "You have to know the rules before you can break them," she said haughtily. "You ready to go?"

"Yup. Need some fresh air," AJ said firmly.

They left the bookstore without exchanging a single word with the young man behind the counter. He'd obviously deemed them not worth his time.

As soon as they got clear of the building (and AJ took several deep breaths of clean ocean air) she said, "I thought you told me that Phoebe Reed was prosperous."

Bea nodded. "That's what I've always thought. That she was too good for the likes of the rest of us, as her bookstore was doing so well."

"That," AJ said, indicating the building behind them, "is not doing well."

"Maybe she has a really good online business," Bea said. "That's how some of the folks in town survive the winter months. Their online stores do as well, if not better, than their brick-and-mortar ones."

"Maybe," AJ said. She doubted it, somehow.

Phoebe Reed's store wasn't prosperous. It was barely limping along on cheap books that no one wanted, or would only pick up if desperate. It wasn't a welcoming place. No community would form around it.

While most of the Bridgewater Inn's business was from tourists, there was still a large contingent of locals who supported the café inside the inn, who regularly came in for breakfast or lunch. They made up at least thirty percent of that part of the business.

Whenever AJ ran a special for tourists, she also tried to run a special for the locals as well. It just made good business sense to keep both sides as happy as possible.

As they got into the car, Bea asked, "Where should I drop you off?"

AJ grinned at the way Bea tried to suppress her eagerness. "Trying to get rid of me, huh? On your last week?"

Bea gave a heavy sigh. "It isn't like that, and you know it. I just...I haven't painted enough today."

"It's okay. I get it. Drop me off to close the inn, I'll walk back to my house from there."

"You sure? I could drive you all the way there," Bea said.

"Yeah, I want the walk. Fresh air and all that," AJ said. Though her clothes really didn't smell of mold, she did want some time to walk and think for herself.

"Only if you promise to go straight home and not check in on the inn, 'just to see how things are going,'" Bea said, still parked and with no intention of going anywhere until AJ had made her promise.

AJ grimaced. Was she that easy to read? Sure, she'd been thinking about it. Taking an entire afternoon *off* just felt... wrong. Decadent, but in a lazy way, not in a virtuous way.

Was decadence ever virtuous?

"Yes, Mom," AJ said after glaring at her little sister for a while. "I will go straight home and not do any more work today."

"Good," Bea said. "Maybe you can try to have another vision or something. See who the killer is. Or who their next victim is going to be."

AJ grimaced at that. "I can't force a vision," she said. "Believe me, I've tried. Ended up with a headache bordering on a migraine." It had been over the summer, while she'd been practicing with her scrying bowl.

"Is that why you can't figure out who killed Gladys?" Bea asked as she finally started the car.

"Yeah," AJ said. "That, and I'm still having an awful time seeing into the past."

To date, all of AJ's visions had been of things to come. Ursula, her mentor, found that surprising. The past, at least according to her, was easier, as it was already set. For AJ, she considered her past to be behind her. She had no desire to look back. Until that changed, chances were, all of her visions would be future facing.

"So what will you do with the rest of the day?" Bea asked as she slowly proceeded back down Main Street.

"Practice my readings, I guess," AJ said.

Bea scowled at her. "An afternoon off means an afternoon *off*. No working on either job." She thought for a moment, then brightened. "I know! I'll drop you off at the Storm Brew Café. Fred is probably there. You should ask him about Phoebe and Reed's Reads."

"That's...actually a good idea," AJ said. Fred was the town gossip, particularly since Dewey had been murdered earlier that spring. Fred supposedly managed one of the local grocery stores, but he never put in any hours there. Instead, he generally held court at one or another of the coffee houses, continually working on The Great American Novel (yes, the words were always capitalized that way when he said them).

Over the summer, AJ had lost track of the number of times he'd rewritten the first few chapters, emphasizing this theme or restructuring the plot. And he'd already been working on that missive for eight years? Ten?

However, Fred might know something about Phoebe and why numbers were going to strangle her.

Give AJ something she could use. Before it was too late.

Chapter Four

AJ SAID her goodbyes and got out of the car across the street from the Storm Brew Café. It was easy to cross the street at this time, as traffic was always lighter during the week. Plus, fewer people were in town overall, particularly as fall approached. In the height of summer, it was like a game of Frogger when someone tried to cross anywhere other than a crosswalk. AJ clutched her raincoat to her as she walked, against the sudden gusts that tried to sneak in and steal her warmth. Perimenopause had really messed with her inner thermometer. Now, she frequently felt cold more intensely than she had when she'd been younger.

Either that, or another of those damned hot flashes would sneak up on her and she'd be sweating. Fortunately, she'd learned to dress for the pacific northwest weather as a kid, which always meant layers.

The Storm Brew Café, like many of the buildings on Main Street, had been someone's residence at some point. Clean black-and-white checked tile covered the floor of the entranceway, all the way from the door to the grand staircase that was roped off, while scratched and scarred wooden floors branched off to the left and right.

To the left stood the counter and a few tables. From there, delicious smells emanated, like grilled cheese and rich coffee. On the right, in what had probably at one time been a formal dining room, were the comfy couches and chairs. The gas fireplace was lit up, warming the area. Fred was on that side, busily scribbling in his notebook, occasionally glancing up at the street, as if seeking someone, *anyone* to distract him from actually having to write.

Even though it was already past noon, AJ decided to pick up a snack as well as a decaf coffee. The café made its own granola and served it with a lovely unsweetened yogurt, which sounded perfect just then.

Juli was behind the counter, as cheerful as ever, the opposite of the Seattle sullen barista. She'd trimmed her dirty blonde hair recently so it no longer fell into her eyes, while the other half of her head was still down to just stubble. Piercings decorated her eyebrow, nose, and lip, and tattoos covered most of her right arm, a full sleeve in progress.

Maybe all those accouterments made her cool enough to be a good barista, to make up for her bright smile and the little heart she'd drawn over the "i" of her nametag.

"What'll be today?" Juli asked brightly.

AJ wondered again what sorts of pharmaceutical aids Juli relied on to remain so determinedly chipper.

"London Fog decaf," AJ said. "And an order of granola."

"You got it!" Juli said.

"How's the sleeve coming along?" AJ asked as Juli started to grind her beans.

"Got most of the scales of the fish filled in," Juli said, beaming. She showed AJ the carp that appeared to be swimming/dancing with a red ribbon, heading down from her elbow to her wrist in some sort of private ritual that only Juli understood. The ribbon was still bright red from when it had been inked at the beginning of summer. Now, the black outline of the carp's scales were mostly filled in with glimmering shades of pink, green, and white.

"Nice," AJ said, nodding.

"You let me know if you ever want to get some ink done," Juli said. "I can get you a deal."

"Thanks," AJ said. "You'll be the first I ask if I ever get that itch."

Six months ago, AJ didn't know she had magic. Didn't expect to be living in a small town. Wasn't about to start up a psychic business.

Never say never had become her personal philosophy.

AJ took her drink and her small bowl over to where Fred was just putting pen and notebook to the side. AJ caught his eye and held up her cup, asking silently if she could join him.

Fred made an entire show about considering her question, whether or not it was a good time for him to break the *flow* of the words.

AJ maintained a polite smile when he finally waved her over, instead of the serious eyeroll he deserved.

"Just taking a short break," Fred informed her. "Been writing for much of the afternoon, actually." He picked up his own coffee cup and took a sip.

Fred's gray eyes glanced curiously at her. His appearance hadn't changed over the six months that AJ had known him: he still had a protruding chin and a forehead that sloped away, with a thin fringe of dark brown hair clinging to the bottom of his shiny white scalp. He wore a nice blue-and-white checked flannel, jeans, and heavy work boots that had never seen a lick of dirt.

AJ just nodded politely and steadfastly did *not* ask him about his writing. She'd be there for the next three hours, unable to get a word in edgewise. Fred could talk a blue streak when it came to writing. At the same time, she'd be surprised if Fred ever managed to finish his Great American Novel.

"So do you have any news for me today? Or just here to ask questions?" Fred said, giving her a smirk.

"A question, actually," AJ said. She glanced around the room, as if to check and make sure that no one was going to overhear her.

That drew Fred in, like a fly to honey. "Do tell," he purred, obviously salivating for anything juicy.

"Bea and I stopped at Reed's Reads earlier today," AJ said. "Now, it was my understanding that Phoebe Reed is quite well off, and that her business was booming. But that shop, well, it didn't strike me as a money maker."

"You're right," Fred said. "That shop? Really. It's an eyesore. You know that Phoebe doesn't go to the Chamber of Commerce meetings anymore, right?"

AJ nodded. She'd never seen Phoebe at them, though she hadn't been to many, just over the summer, once a month.

"Some of the members took her to task about a year

ago, shaming her for the condition of her store," Fred said smugly. "I heard there was quite a row."

"Interesting," AJ said. She bet that Bea hadn't attended that meeting, and so hadn't heard about it. It must have happened during the winter months, and Bea only attended meetings during the summer. "So how is she making her money? Online store?"

"No one knows," Fred said with a sly grin.

"Not even you?" AJ asked. "You know everything that happens in this town."

"True, true," Fred said. "Though I didn't know you had psychic powers," he said, giving her a quick glare.

"What do you mean?" AJ said, ready to deny them.

"You're reopening Ursula's psychic business this weekend," Fred said. "I saw the ad you took out."

"Oh," was all that AJ could say. Though the newspaper wasn't supposed to come out until the next day, she wasn't surprised that Fred had already seen a copy.

"Did you have some sort of vision about Phoebe? Or the bookstore?" Fred asked, studying her keenly.

AJ had never been good at lying. Bea was much better at it than she'd ever been.

"Something like that," was all that AJ replied. She didn't have to tell him the full truth.

"Ooooh," Fred said. His eyes gleamed. "I can see I'm going to have to stay on your good side, if I want the early scoop."

AJ couldn't help herself. She snorted at him. "That's assuming that the vision I have makes any damned sense."

Fred just nodded sagely. "Yes, that's the life of an artist.

Interpreting symbols, trying to give meaning to signs hauled up into the open by your subconscious."

AJ gave Fred a curious look. "Artist?" she said. "No, my sister Bea's the artist."

Fred waved his hand in the air, as if scattering all her words. "Being a psychic, in touch with the deeper world, means you're an artist too. Maybe you need to spend more time immersing yourself in the world of symbols, so you can more readily determine the meaning of what you see."

AJ blinked, then blinked some more. "Like the tarot cards," she said slowly. "Those are all symbols, not words."

"Exactly like that!" Fred said, nodding. "They operate at a deeper level in the brain, the part that recognizes pictures, and speaks directly to that, long before the thinking, language levels of the brain engage."

"Huh," was all AJ had to say in response. She'd never thought of it like that.

She thought about her conversation as she walked home from the café.

Ursula was all about getting in touch with spirits and magic. Maybe AJ should instead start thinking about how the pictures on the cards related to psychological symbols, things that her clients were likely to bring to the table.

Wouldn't that make her a fraud, though? If she wasn't tapping into something deeper?

Or did just understanding the psychology of the images mean she was going deep enough?

Though AJ wasn't certain she agreed with Fred, she couldn't stop wondering about whether or not she might, indeed, be an artist. Unsurprisingly, all her readings were completely thrown off that night. She couldn't call up a damned thing because she was too much in her own head.

Which wasn't going to work at all, particularly given that in just two days, she was going to have to start giving readings and actually *work* with clients.

She went to bed frustrated.

In the morning, the local town app's notifications were all taken up with the fact that Phoebe Reed had been found dead.

Shot in the parking lot of her store. Not strangled.

Chapter Five

A FEELING of dread filled AJ as she walked up to the inn that morning.

It had nothing to do with the nice day outside. The morning had dawned clear and cool, without a cloud in sight, but the sunlight couldn't brighten her dark mood. Waves lapped far off shore, the tide all the way out. It wouldn't come back in until late that afternoon. She didn't miss the water—it was right there—but she still felt as though a friend had taken a step away from her. Long-legged terns raced along beside her, stopping now and again to peck at the sand, searching futilely for their breakfast. Even the wind tried to hold her back, blowing fiercely against her side.

The somber red brick of the Bridgewater Inn looked as solid as any fortress. Gray concrete pillars holding up a mock portico felt like bars. Ornate gables rose from the third story of the building in sharp triangles across the front, like fangs ready to drop down on someone's unsuspecting head.

At least the yard had held onto its lush, summer green, though that too was fading, given the number of dead and dying leaves on the roses and other shrubs. More than one car stood in the circular driveway in front of the building, their owners having abandoned them, at least temporarily.

AJ's mood didn't get any better after she walked into the inn. There weren't any guests waiting in the lobby, filling up the black-and-white marble tile floor. The chandeliers still shone down cheerfully in the large space. Delicious scents of perfectly toasted bread and roasted coffee drifted out from the café.

However, Willow sat behind the reception desk that morning, and her glare could have turned any living thing that dared to approach her to stone. She wore her usual outfit: a men's white dress shirt that had been tailored to her thin frame and a vintage black vest that looked chic instead of old-fashioned. Like Juli, one half of her head had been shaved down to stubble, while the other half was a red not found in nature. All the necklaces she wore around her neck, like talismans, didn't appear to have warded off evil or made her way any easier that day.

Guiltily, AJ remembered that in addition to Phoebe's death, the paper had come out that morning, with her ad about the grand reopening of Ursula's psychic business. Willow claimed to be a witch, though according to Ursula, the girl had no magical power whatsoever.

"Good morning, Willow!" AJ said, determined to be cheery.

Willow's look was so cold the temperature in the lobby fell a few degrees.

"So you're a psychic, now, too?" Willow demanded.

AJ shrugged. "It was part of the agreement, when I bought the house from Ursula. That I continue with her psychic business." She lowered her voice. "I'm a little nervous about opening up everything this weekend. But Ursula said that it was time." AJ sighed, then feeling horrifically manipulative, said, "Do you have any advice for keeping myself, not purified after dealing with clients, but separated?"

It was something that Ursula had talked about, how AJ was going to need to develop her own ritual to refresh herself after allowing people into her home.

Ursula might have said it using a lot more woo-woo words and talking about her spirit and sacred blah-de-blah. It had taken a while for AJ to understand what her mentor had been trying to get at. It wasn't necessarily about the magic or her spirit, but letting people into her home, then reclaiming the space, making it hers, afterward.

"Oh," Willow said, obviously taken back. She'd probably been expecting AJ to be defensive, not asking for help. "Sure," she said after a few moments. "You should probably burn sage to clean the extra energies out of the air. And maybe get some selenite, or some amber, to help release those spirits as well."

"Thanks! I'll do that," AJ said with a smile. "How's the morning been?"

"Slow," Willow admitted. "Though everyone's who's come in here for coffee has wanted to know about Phoebe Reed."

"I saw that!" AJ said. "Horrible, isn't it?"

"It is," Willow said solemnly. "Though I knew something was going to happen today." She held up one of the stones tangling from her necklaces. "The black topaz was speaking to me this morning. It's been extra warm, trying to take in all the negativity and filter it away from me."

"Do you know anything about Phoebe Reed?" AJ asked, trying to steer the conversation away from Willow's more esoteric beliefs. It was either that, or roll her eyes so hard she'd hurt something.

"She was a cougar," Willow said.

At AJ's blank expression, Willow elaborated. "Always hitting on younger men. Generally only hired young men to run her shop. Was always flirting with them, or getting them to move boxes of books around to show off their muscles."

"Eww," AJ said. "Do you think one of them was angry enough with her to kill her?"

Willow shrugged. "No idea. But I'll meditate on it tonight, see if the moon will bring enlightenment. The Goddess has been strangely silent about the killing, though."

"You did say you felt as though something bad was going to happen today," AJ said, trying not to let her guilt overcome her. She knew she shouldn't encourage the girl.

"True, but it wasn't enough. I couldn't do anything about just a feeling, you know?" Willow said, obviously frustrated.

"I totally get you," AJ said. "You need anything? Coffee? Potty break?"

"Naw, I'm good," Willow said. She sighed, the glare returning. "I really wanted to hate you, you know. Running your own psychic business has always been a dream of mine."

AJ shrugged. "I'm going to be dealing with people, in my home, on a regular basis," she reminded the girl. "It isn't going to be all kittens and kisses."

"True," Willow said. After a moment, her lop-sided grin replacing the scowl. "And dealing with the spirit world is no picnic either."

"True," AJ said, though she and Willow had very different ideas of what that meant.

"I'll see you later," AJ said after a few moments. "Text me if you need anything."

"Thanks," Willow said. She still sounded pissed off, though to a much lesser extent.

One crisis averted, AJ walked into the next one when she entered the hallway leading to the office. It was covered in wood paneling, a poor design choice from the remodel of the 1970s. The temperature dropped precipitously as she rounded the corner, before she reached the office door.

"Good morning, Gladys," AJ said, greeting the ghost who haunted the inn. Normally, Gladys saved all her energy to speak with AJ and not frost the place.

Was she angry about something?

No one greeted AJ. No presence made itself known though.

With a shrug, AJ walked into the office. She'd changed it around a lot since taking it over from Irv and Eva.

There used to be two desks in the middle of the room, facing one another, as the husband-and-wife team worked together to run the inn. AJ had gotten rid of Irv's desk (too many bad associations, honestly, particularly after he'd tried to kill her) and had pushed Eva's against the wall, so that one side of it was pressed against the large window that looked over the garden.

That way, AJ could either look at her marvelous view, or look straight ahead, and not be bothered by whatever was going on outside.

She'd left some of the pictures on the walls—photos from the inn's past, including a couple of Irv and Eva when they'd first bought the place. She'd also put up a piece of her sister's art and one of her favorite pictures of her and Bea, as kids, giggling hard while in the middle of blowing bubbles at a family picnic. A couple of soap bubbles floated in the foreground, stealing the focus, leaving the sisters blurry. AJ didn't remember the event. However, there was no denying the joy the pair of them were sharing, captured perfectly in that moment.

No ghostly figure awaited AJ as she walked into the room. However, a cold wind rattled the pictures on the wall. AJ had followed Eva's example and used cheap frames as well as plastic covers, not glass. Though Gladys didn't knock the pictures off the wall regularly, it happened often enough that AJ didn't want to have to worry about broken glass.

"What is it? What's wrong?" AJ asked. She still felt a little awkward talking to an "empty" room, and was glad that no one worked with her in the office.

The sense she got was one of frustration.

"I did go to the historical society yesterday," AJ pointed out. "Read up on all of the supposed sightings of you. I've been trying to learn more of your history."

A sigh went through the room. AJ could hear the disappointment in it.

"I know," she said, trying to placate the ghost. "I didn't find out much. But I am trying." The last thing she needed that day was an angry ghost.

A rush of wind blew at her, as strong as any that regularly came off the ocean.

A single word came with it.

Vision.

"Now, Gladys, you know I've tried," AJ said. She'd explained that she couldn't see into the past. Nor should she ever force a vision.

Try.

AJ rolled her eyes. "I will," she said. "Later."

A picture suddenly fell from the wall. Then another. And another. Even the piece of artwork from her sister rattled ominously, something that Gladys hadn't done before.

"You want me to try right now," AJ said.

She knew what would happen. She wouldn't see anything *and* she'd be plagued with a bad headache for the rest of the day. She had *work* to do, bills to pay, schedules to review, damn it!

However, she also had the feeling that Gladys wasn't about to leave her alone until she attempted a vision.

"All right, all right," AJ grumbled. "Fine."

She had a true scrying bowl in her house, a lovely hand-blown glass piece, mostly clear, with swirls of blue and green running along the sides.

All she had here was a bowl she'd borrowed from the inn's café. It was white, with an inch-wide flat rim running along the top, made up of small brown rectangles, with beige circles and squares inside. Yet another piece from the 1970s, though not chic enough to be called vintage.

AJ filled the bowl from her own water bottle, the one she now carried with her most of the time, that was laced with electrolytes because her body had grown weird and needed more minerals to keep away the headaches perimenopause brought.

After carefully placing the bowl in the center of her clean desk, AJ picked up a couple of binder clips and held them loosely in one hand. At home, she had a jar full of beautifully polished stones that she used. Really, though, she just needed something that she could drop into the water to break the vision if it grew too strong or threatening.

AJ stared into the bowl, noting idly that some of the trim had been scratched. They needed to replace all the servings. While the inn was doing well, it wasn't doing that well. Maybe she'd have to set up a separate fund for that sort of maintenance...

With a sigh, AJ brought her thoughts back to what she was supposedly doing, namely, having a vision about Gladys's murder.

What had happened, so long ago? Over one hundred years in the past, at this point. Who was Gladys? Why had she been killed? Who had done it? Why?

AJ felt the world around her slow down, which was always a good sign. Gladys's presence filled the room, the solid sense that someone was there with AJ, though she couldn't see anyone. The temperature dropped, and AJ had goosebumps crisscrossing her shoulders and down her arms. When white mists rose from the surface of the water, she wondered if the room had gotten so cold that she was seeing steam.

The weight of the ghost bore down on her shoulders. AJ shivered, pain spiking through her forehead. Pressure built behind her eyes. The air smelled of stale ice.

What, was Gladys *willing* AJ to have a vision? How could she do that?

There was just so much about the supernatural world that AJ didn't understand, that no one appeared to know about.

After a few moments, AJ opened herself up to the experience instead of struggling against it.

Ice seemed to flow through her, her blood growing sluggish. Her own breath came out foggy. Though her skin was already pale, her hands turned bright white as she was pushed along, further into the magic, into that nether place where visions came from.

The mists dancing across the water in the bowl didn't clear. They didn't drop away, showing a mirror underneath.

Instead, the white mists solidified, slowly forming into a box. No, it was more irregular than that. Piece by piece, the image formed. The white gave way to spreading color.

Books. Old books. Ancient, actually. AJ could practically smell the mold coming off the pages.

Three of them. All hardbacks. No dust jackets. The largest was at the bottom. Words had been printed on the spines, but they had long ago been worn off.

A leather strap was buckled around the books, making them into a solid bundle. The largest of the three books was about ten inches tall and seven inches wide. But AJ could feel the weight of the bundle, how the strap bit into the palm of her hand when she carried them.

Or was that a feeling from Gladys? Had these been her books?

Yessss came the hissed word.

AJ had no idea why this pile of books was important. The top book had a faded blue cloth cover, the next, brown, and the bottom one had been yellow at some point. But she had no idea what the subject matter of any of the books had been. Were they children's books? School books?

She started to lift her hand from the desk, the one with the clips in it, to drop into the water to scatter the mist and the image.

However, the vision wasn't done yet. A second piece coalesced beside the stack of books, slowly unfolding. While the colors of the books were muted, this part of AJ's vision was a vibrant green, eventually taking the shape of a four-leaf clover.

Again, AJ felt Gladys's approval.

Yet another cold wind blew through the office, this time, dissipating the images floating over the scrying bowl AJ had been using.

Thank you, came the whispered words.

Then Gladys was gone. AJ shivered again as warmth flooded back into her limbs.

What the hell? What did a stack of books and a four-leaf clover have to do with anything?

The pressure returned behind AJ's eyes, her temples starting to beat out a rhythm of pain. Swell. Now, on top of everything else, she had a headache the size of the ocean pounding down on her.

She knew she should be excited. She had the feeling that she'd just had a breakthrough. She'd seen something from the past instead of always looking into the future.

However, she had no idea what it meant. No clue how it related to Gladys. Plus, now she had a horrible headache that no modern medication could touch.

With a sigh, AJ picked up the bowl, intending on dumping it out in the restroom sink next door.

Of course, she ended up spilling water all over her desk.

She didn't want to ask what else could go wrong that day because she was afraid that the world might just show her how bad it could get.

Chapter Six

BECAUSE IT WAS STILL a new-to-her habit, AJ occasionally felt guilty taking her entire lunch break—a full hour—just to eat and rest.

Not that day.

She couldn't count the number of things that had gone wrong that morning, including Payne coming to her and bitching about needing to replace the water filters on the spa again, Rosita complaining about the lack of guests starting the first week of October, and even Willow shooting daggers at her whenever she went out into the lobby.

AJ rushed back to her house, intending to lie down and rest for the entire hour. She tried to no longer eat on the run when it came to her meals. She could make an exception that day.

Since starting into perimenopause, she'd had many more headaches than she'd used to. Fortunately, Bea had given her something that helped: flannel pillows, with tiny beans in them, that AJ kept in her freezer. On a headache day, being able to lie down with one of those on her forehead really helped.

AJ had just shut her eyes and breathed a sigh of relief as the coolness from the bag started penetrating when her phone rang.

Because, of course it did.

So few people called her. AJ groggily picked it up, sighing again when she saw it wasn't spam but actually her sister.

"Hello?" AJ said as she laid back down, trying to rearrange the delightfully cold pillow across her entire forehead and eyes while keeping her phone tucked in against her ear.

"I take it you saw the news," Bea said.

"Yup," AJ said. "Phoebe Reed was shot."

"I thought your vision showed her being strangled," Bea said. She sounded cross.

"It showed her dead," AJ said bluntly. "With a string of numbers wrapped around her throat."

"Maybe she was having money problems," Bea said. "Which would explain the numbers around her neck, even though she was shot."

"Maybe?" AJ said. "I have no idea."

"Well, what's your next step?" Bea said. "Have another vision?"

"Already did," AJ said with a grimace. She explained her strange morning, being forced into a vision by a ghost. Or something like that.

"Oh," Bea said. "Where are you?"

"I'm at home," AJ replied. She didn't feel like giving her

little sister all the details of her massive headache. She could take care of herself.

"Are you OK?" Bea said. "You sound a bit off."

AJ sighed. She should have known that Bea would figure out something. "I'm fine. I'm actually lying down."

"You're taking a break? As part of your lunch break? How sick are you, really?" Bea insisted.

"I'm fine," AJ insisted.

Bea snorted at her. "No, you're not. You're my over-achieving older sister who would work diligently doing something she hated until she dropped over dead."

AJ was quiet for a few moments, thinking. "I think—I hope—that's an outdated description of me."

"Who are you and what have you done with my sister?" Bea demanded.

It was AJ's turn to snort.

"No, I get it. You really have been making an effort to be different than who you were, to change. I need to remember that." Bea said. She paused, then added, "But what are you going to do about Phoebe?"

"I don't know," AJ said. "Maybe have another vision? See if I can see the killer? Just...not today."

"All right," Bea said. "I'll leave you alone. I am glad that you're at least trying to take care of yourself. Should I bring you some soup or something?"

AJ really wanted to say yes. She wondered what the soup of the day was from the Storm Brew Café, and if it would pair well with a grilled cheese sandwich.

However, that felt like giving up too much of her independence. It was just a headache.

"No, I'll grab something quick to eat on my way back to the inn," AJ said instead.

"How about we do dinner, then?" Bea said. "I'll bring something over, so you don't have to face anyone. And that way, you won't have to cook either."

"Thank you," AJ said, feeling the gratitude flowing up all the way from the bottom of her soul.

The sisters hung up and AJ tossed her phone to the side, readjusting the cold pillow on her face.

It was nice to have an adult relationship with her sister these days. She wasn't looking forward to Bea leaving after the weekend. Not that AJ couldn't handle being here on her own. She'd come to rely, though, on the support of her sister.

And her company. She feared the long cold months ahead, and being all alone.

She'd burn that bridge when she came to it. For now, she could rest. Recharge. Then go out and conquer the rest of her day.

Chapter Seven

FRIDAY CAME and AJ was no closer to figuring out who'd killed Phoebe Reed. Remnants of her headache from the day before remained, like a particularly nasty hangover.

Which honestly, was the last thing AJ needed.

Supposedly, that night, actually, in just a short while, was the grand re-opening of the psychic business.

Ursula had put in some calls to her past clients, urging them to go and visit AJ sometime over the weekend. AJ had put up an ad in the local newspaper that came out on Thursdays, as well as on the town app, advertising free fifteen-minute consults.

Would anyone show up? AJ had no idea.

She'd paid for a banner that she'd hung over the door, announcing that she was open again. She'd replaced the sign out front with one of her own design. It was still hokey, but it felt more like her. Instead of an open palm with rays streaming from it, she had a crystal ball, supported by waves, with light surrounding it. She'd kept most of Usrula's wording, though, just removing the palm reading because she'd discovered that she had no aptitude for that whatsoever.

Tarot Cards
Divinations
No question too trivial to be considered!

She'd also kept the neon purple sign for the front window that said PSYCHIC!

AJ found her hands shaking as she walked through the front rooms, making sure that everything was set up. The white and black tile had been polished until it shone, particularly given the new lights AJ had installed. She'd painted the walls a brighter white, opening up the space, so it wasn't so dim and crowded.

The tower directly to the right side of the door still had elegant benches that curved around the edges, with pegs above them for coats. The table with business cards had been downgraded from a card table to a chic end table, which took up much less space and actually came from this century. A clipboard also sat on the table, encouraging people to sign up for AJ's newsletter, which she really was going to have to start this weekend. If anyone signed up for it. She'd already created the website, as Ursula hadn't had any online presence at all.

AJ had taken down all the myriad pictures and sent those to Ursula, leaving the walls more bare than she liked. However, that was a problem for another day. For now, the lobby felt clean, open, and inviting, instead of claustrophobic and vaguely threatening.

A grand staircase swept along the inside of one wall,

leading up to the second floor. AJ had removed the carpet and refinished the wood, so instead of looking ratty and dark, it now looked sleek and modern. She'd added a rope across the bottom of it, as she really didn't want the curious going up the stairs and poking around the more private parts of her house.

A white, modern, accordion door now closed off the kitchen from the entranceway, instead of the curtains that Ursula had put up ages ago. AJ had also put in a sliding barndoor to shut the reading room off from the hallway. The restroom was still under the stairs, just a toilet and a sink. AJ had redone the floor in there with a beautiful sea-green tile, leaving the beaded wainscoting, though painting it white, so the tiny area no longer felt cramped.

AJ looked around again. Everything was in place. Everything was all set.

She'd built it. Would they come?

Her phone chirped a reminder that it was now time.

AJ made herself walk over to the front door and open it, intending on turning over the "closed" sign hanging in the middle of it to "open."

She had *not* expected there to be people out there.

A lot of people.

Wow.

They stood in a line that went down the stairs, out the gate of the garden, and stretched along the sidewalk there.

She nearly slammed the door shut in shock.

After mentally picking her jaw up off the floor, she waved at everyone then flipped the sign over. "It's a good night for readings!" she called out, hoping that she didn't sound as weirded out as she felt.

That got her several laughs as well as a few, "Yays!"

Before AJ could turn to her first client—a woman she'd never seen before—Bea came bustling up the stairs, passing everyone.

"Sorry! I'm late! Sorry, sorry!" Bea said, thrusting a bouquet of flowers out at AJ.

Of course, Bea was late. She was never on time for anything.

"What are you doing here?" AJ asked.

"I'm here to help!" Bea said, beaming at her. "Help you wrangle the crowd."

AJ opened her mouth to tell Bea that she didn't need any help, then snapped it shut again. "Thank you," she said instead.

Fortunately, the bouquet that Bea had brought came with its own vase, so AJ didn't have to go searching for one. She placed it on the end table, happy for the cheer that it brought to the place.

"You ready?" Bea asked, still standing at the front door, not allowing anyone else to come into the entranceway yet.

AJ walked over to the barn door hiding the reading room, sliding it open. "As ready as I'll ever be," she said.

AJ had made the most changes to the reading room. She'd removed all the cheap purple cloth covering the walls, added sconces she could dim, as well as painted the room a light, soothing, blue-green color. She kept her scrying bowl in here, along with a pitcher of fresh water, just in case.

She'd actually taken Willow's advice and bought herself a ball of selenite from the local gem and mineral shop. It sat on the table which separated her from her client. It looked pretty. AJ hadn't had any *feelings* from it beyond satisfaction, and she doubted she ever would.

The table was the same one Ursula had used. Under the ugly tablecloth that AJ had happily burned she'd found a sturdy oak piece with beautifully carved legs and sides. Ursula had gifted it to her, saying she didn't need any of the furniture from the house, just the pictures, linens, and clothes.

The woman AJ had briefly seen standing on the front porch came bustling in, all smiles. "Hi there! I'm Agnes," she said, though she turned the "s" into a "sh" sound. She slid the door shut behind her. "Ursula told me all about you, and insisted that I go see you as soon as you were open!"

"Thank you! I really appreciate it," AJ said. And she did.

Agnes had a flat face, with blue-gray eyes peering out over her pink cheeks. Sandy blonde hair hung down all around her face, like straw that had been conditioned within an inch of its life. Her body was solid, her hands possibly bigger and stronger than Roland's. The collar and cuffs of her coat were frayed around the edges, and the scarf she wore was obviously handmade.

This wasn't a woman of means, AJ was certain. She'd have to try to remember her name, and ask Ursula about her later.

AJ tugged the tarot cards over and shuffled them. "Do you have a question for me today?"

Agnes nodded eagerly. "I do! It's—"

"Don't tell me," AJ insisted, holding up one hand. "I don't want to know."

Agnes blinked, surprised at this change in routine.

"Think about your question while I'm shuffling the cards," AJ directed. "Think long and hard about it."

She shuffled three more times, then placed the deck in front of Agnes. "Cut the cards, still thinking about your question."

Agnes gave her a sly smile, then tapped the top of the deck, declining to mix the cards up more.

"Very well," AJ said. "I'm going to do a three-card draw. The first card represents the past, the second is the present, and the third is all about the future. Are you ready?"

"Yes!" Agnes said, giving her a great grin.

"Let's begin."

Chapter Eight

AJ DROPPED her head down onto the table with a thunk. "Is that it?" she said, her voice a moan.

"That's it," Bea said softly. "That's the lot of them."

AJ shook her head. She could barely lift it.

Who knew that reading people's fortunes for almost three hours straight would completely exhaust her? She certainly hadn't.

"Thank you for helping," she said to Bea. "Really. I have no idea how I'd have managed without you."

"You're welcome," Bea said, beaming at her. "You might need to hire help the next time you decide to offer such a bargain, like the free readings."

AJ groaned. "Never. I'm never doing this again."

"Uhm, I hate to be the one to point this out to you, but you are scheduled to do it again tomorrow night."

AJ gave a louder groan. "Just shoot me now. Please. Put me out of my misery."

"How about instead, you follow me to the kitchen? I'll

pour you a glass of wine and see if there's anything edible in your fridge," Bea countered.

"Fine," AJ said, still feeling as though their roles were reversed, with her being the bratty younger sister and Bea being older and taking care of her.

AJ had kept the original configuration of the kitchen, with its tiny stove next to the entranceway, along with the apartment-sized refrigerator that was shorter than she was but suited her needs. However, she'd replaced all the appliances with modern versions, laid down new linoleum that was white with a confetti pattern of pastel blues and greens, repainted the cabinets white and the walls a sage green, and put in a larger sink. She'd kept the table and two chairs that Ursula had used, as they were comfy and fit perfectly.

"Go stick your head under the water," Bea directed AJ as she started rifling through the fridge.

With a sigh of relief, AJ went to do just that. She kept an extra towel right next to the sink, just so she could dunk her hair and not worry about it.

With the water pouring down around her ears, AJ couldn't hear anything that Bea was saying to her. That was fine, Bea could talk with her in a few moments.

The water washed away much of the night's work, cleansing her soul and, okay, maybe her aura as well. She felt lighter and fresher than she had for the past couple of days when she wrapped the towel around her head.

"That's better," AJ said.

Bea just shook her head. "Weirdo."

AJ rolled her eyes. It was something the sisters were never going to agree on. Bea thought the only place to wash one's hair was in the shower, never in the sink. AJ had put in the larger kitchen sink just so she could get her whole head wet.

"So what did you find in the fridge?" AJ asked. She thought she had some chicken left? Maybe some grapes? She was suddenly ravenous.

"You go sit and I'll bring it to you. I take it you didn't hear what I was saying?" Bea said.

AJ gratefully sat down. "Nope. Water running in my ears."

"While people were waiting their turn in the lobby, I might have asked a few leading questions about Phoebe Reed," Bea said with a grin.

"What's the gossip?" AJ said.

"According to more than one of our illustrious locals, Phoebe Reed was not only a bookseller, but a book*keeper*," Bea said. "Her side gig, and how she managed to stay afloat, was that she worked as an accountant. She wasn't a full CPA. But she did taxes for people around here for years."

"Huh," AJ said, sitting back in her chair as Bea bustled about her small kitchen. "That would explain the numbers around her neck. It was probably one of her accountant clients who killed her."

"Exactly! That's what I thought!" Bea said. She beamed at AJ as she carried the cutting board over to the table, covered with "deconstructed salad"—cut cucumbers, a pile of carrot and celery sticks, cherry tomatoes, cauliflower florets, and some pickled beets. A second plate contained small pieces of meat from the rotisserie chicken Bea had brought over the other day.

Bea set those down on the table with a flourish, then went back and poured them both a large glass of a delicious smoky red wine.

"Here's to a successful first night in business!" Bea proposed as a toast, lifting her glass.

"Here, here," AJ said, beaming at her sister. She fell to eating, despite how late at night it was. Only after she'd managed to stuff half of what her sister had served did AJ finally look up.

"Was tonight successful?" AJ asked after a few moments. "I did give away readings for free all night."

"Hold that thought," Bea said, standing up and leaving the kitchen. When she came back in, she held AJ's scrying bowl and the clipboard.

"I encouraged people to sign up for your newsletter," Bea said smugly, sliding the clipboard over to AJ.

There were almost two full pages worth of names.

"Okay," AJ said. Now, what was she going to say to all these people? She'd have to figure out something. But at least it was the start of a client base.

"I also put out a tip bowl," Bea said, handing AJ her scrying bowl.

"Uhm, thank you?" AJ said, unsure what to do with it. There were a lot of one-dollar bills, a couple of fives, and at least one ten that she could see. Plus change that rattled in the bottom of the bowl.

On the one hand, she was incredibly grateful that Bea had thought of it.

On the other hand, this was her *scrying* bowl. She'd never been one for woo-woo emotions and like that, but it felt as though her primary tool had just been polluted.

She'd have to do something about it later. What, exactly, she wasn't certain.

Willow would surely have an idea. She'd have to remember to ask her.

In fact, if she ever ran another special deal like this, she'd have to ask Willow if she'd like to work with AJ on it, particularly if Bea was out of town.

After eating a little more, AJ finally felt settled back into her body. For a while, it had felt as though her head was a balloon, floating way above her.

"Thank you so much for coming by," AJ told Bea. "I'm not sure what I would have done without you tonight."

Bea gave her a grin.

"I know," she said. "You would never think to ask for help." She sighed, and grew more serious. "It's something you're going to have to get used to, particularly living here, in a small town. People rely on each other in Milltown, much more so than in a big city like Seattle. They're going to come by and ask for help. And expect you to do the same. If you don't, people will start to think you're too snooty."

"Message received," AJ said. She'd already experienced that a little. There was a "friends and family" rate at the inn that they used whenever a town local brought family in to stay. She'd been a little surprised by it. Eva had told her that was just the way things worked.

"So who were Phoebe Reed's accounting clients?" AJ asked after another sip of wine.

Bea's expression turned sour. "No one knew. Or would admit to it," she said. "It appeared to be common knowledge that she worked as an accountant/bookkeeper.

However, no one claimed to be a client of hers, or knowing any of her clients."

"That's strange," AJ said. "How did she stay in business if she didn't have any clients?"

"Oh, I think she had clients. I just think nobody wanted to admit to it," Bea said. "She wasn't the nicest person. No one, at least no one I spoke with this evening, was mourning her passing."

AJ thought for a few moments. "The police will know all this, right? Whoever's assigned to the case? They'll find her list of clients, and will question them."

"Yes," Bea said slowly. "I suppose."

"What?" AJ said. "Just because I saw her die before she did doesn't mean I have to solve her murder. Let the police earn their pay."

"And if the killer strikes again? And you didn't do anything?" Bea challenged.

AJ sighed. "Okay. You're right. I'd feel horribly guilty." As she had after Warren's death, when she'd tried to unsuccessfully warn Dewey that he was next.

"Last time, you encouraged yourself to have a vision, to see who the next victim would be," Bea said. "Think you could do that again?"

"Not tonight," AJ said. "There's nothing there. I don't have anything left."

"You used up all your magic?" Bea teased.

"You could say that," AJ agreed.

Bea looked surprised. "Really? Were you doing magic tonight when you were reading? But you weren't using water!"

"I know," AJ said. She blew out a breath. "It's really

hard to explain. I dropped down into the flow of...*something*. The cards were just a touchpoint. The symbols spoke for themselves."

More than one client had been a little taken back by how accurate AJ had been. They said that she used the exact same words and phrases that they had used, themselves, when describing the situation or framing their question.

"Okay," Bea said after a moment. "That explains it."

"Explains what?"

Bea gave AJ her evil little sister grin. "People kept coming out saying that you were good. Scary good. Like, burn-at-the-stake-witchy good."

"Oh," AJ said. "That's...good?"

"It is," Bea said. "Now, you get some rest. Sleep in tomorrow. Take the day off. Because you're going to have to do this all again tomorrow."

"Swell," AJ said, plopping her head back down on the table.

Bea let herself out and AJ just sat there, pondering.

Ursula had been right. AJ was a "natural" at this. She could probably keep herself afloat with only the psychic business, as scary a thought as that might be.

She recognized her fear for what it was: being dependent on a lot of individuals for her income instead of having a job and a faceless employer. Though Rosita and her family had bought the inn, so her employer was anything but faceless.

However, she didn't have to make that jump just yet. The inn still needed her. She hadn't worked her way out of that job, despite already being able to cut down her hours.

AJ washed the late dinner plates, put them on the rack,

made herself some decaf tea, then took herself off to bed. She didn't need to solve anything more complicated than falling asleep, at least for the night.

Chapter Nine

SATURDAY NIGHT TURNED out to be a repeat of Friday night, with a huge crowd all waiting for their free reading. AJ would swear that she'd seen at least half of Milltown grace her reading room that weekend. She'd also set up a calendar, where people could start making appointments with her, though she was charging for those meetings.

She'd thought she'd charged a lot. Then when Bea showed her all booked up for the next several weeks, both on Wednesday afternoons and the weekends, AJ considered raising her prices.

However, there was also Agnes who'd come back and who'd scheduled time with her every other week.

AJ was going to have to work out some sort of sliding scale for people like Agnes. Who, she suspected, was lonely and primarily wanted regular contact with someone, and was willing to pay for it, whether she could afford it or not.

AJ took Sunday off, sleeping in late, taking a long bath, trying to recover. She'd taken her scrying bowl out to the ocean and rinsed it in salt water. That had cleansed it, at least as far as her minuscule woo-woo feelings were concerned.

All Sunday afternoon, AJ tried to work up the enthusiasm to look into her scrying bowl, to see if she could figure out who the killer was, if there would be a next victim. With just thirty minutes before she was to meet Bea for dinner, AJ finally sat herself down in her reading room, filled the bowl with water, picked up a few of the smooth pebbles from her jar, and got herself ready.

"Who killed Phoebe Reed? Who is the next victim? Who is the killer?"

She repeated the words over and over again, trying different variations, but nothing came. No mists clouded the waters, time never slowed down, and AJ never felt herself drop down into that stream, as she had when she'd been doing readings for people.

As soon as the first twinge of a headache started, AJ stopped, sitting back in her chair and sighing.

She wasn't sure why, exactly. Looking into the past was always excruciatingly difficult for her. The only time she'd managed it was when Gladys had forced the issue, and she'd felt awful for a couple of days afterward. So asking about who'd killed Phoebe Reed was probably useless.

However, as AJ didn't catch a glimpse of the next person to die, perhaps the killer was finished. Maybe there wasn't a next victim. Maybe it was a one-and-done deal.

Or perhaps her powers hadn't recovered yet from all the readings she'd done on both Friday and Saturday night.

At least she'd be able to tell Bea she'd tried, and not have her sister plaguing her all evening.

Bea hadn't found anyone who'd admit to being a client

of Phoebe Reed's. She did suggest that AJ ask Fred the next time she saw him.

The sisters said a cheery goodbye. Though they'd grown closer that summer than they'd ever been, even as kids, Bea was looking forward to going back to Seattle to spend the winter with her husband, Peter. The pair of them would be down again in a few weeks.

AJ had told her sister that she'd check in on Bea's cottage, though it wasn't really necessary. Bea had a company who would keep a regular eye on it.

Monday afternoon, AJ went to the Storm Brew Café for lunch, hoping to run into Fred and ask him if he knew anything about Phoebe Reed's accounting business.

However, he wasn't in his usual spot by the window. He was probably at one of the other coffee shops, still "working" on his novel. AJ didn't feel like looking for him. She'd see him at some other time.

Instead, she saw Roland sitting there, by himself, just starting his own lunch. He had an old book open next to his plate, but he looked up when she came into the eating area.

AJ hesitated even as he waved her over. She remembered how angry he'd first looked when Phoebe Reed had come into the historic society building.

Was he the killer?

Roland wore his usual flannel, this time a more colorful shirt, done in blue and white checks. It looked comfy and warm, particularly given the rain that had appeared that morning. He looked much the same, with the full beard, soft eyes, and happy smile.

Okay, so maybe Bea had a point. He was cute. That didn't mean he was innocent.

"Hi there," AJ said brightly. "I wanted to thank you for sending your ghost tour visitors to my place for readings."

A lot of people who'd shown up were strangers, tourists, who'd all come from Roland's tour. It was the perfect opening for chatting with him, as well.

"You're welcome!" Roland said, beaming at her. "Please, join me for lunch."

"If you're certain," AJ said, still hesitant. He couldn't really be a killer, could he? Then again, this would be a good time to chat with him, in a public place, with lots of other people around.

"Of course," Roland said, moving his own dishes to the side as well as putting his book away so that there was room for AJ's own soup and sandwich.

"What were you reading?" AJ asked as she sat down.

"Just an old history book," Roland said, "about the ships that used to run up and down the coast."

"Local history?" AJ said, taking her first taste of the divine clam chowder that Miguel had whipped up that day, savoring the saltiness of it, letting the cream linger on her tongue.

"Sort of," Roland said. "I've also been looking to see if I can find anything more about the inn for you."

"Thank you," AJ said, touched. "Have you been successful?"

"Not really," Roland said. "I've already read most of that material, and I haven't been able to find anything new." He paused, taking a bite of his own sandwich, before he asked, "Have you heard anything more from the ghost?"

AJ peered at him. He seemed eager.

"Why would you want to know?"

He spread his large hands wide as he shrugged, aiming for nonchalance and missing it by a mile. "It's a ghost. Who was alive in the past. Just think of the stories she must know! What she's seen!"

AJ grimaced. "She doesn't have that much recall," she said. "She can't tell me who murdered her. Or even if she's the daughter or the wife."

"But she talks with you?" Roland asked enthusiastically. "You can ask her questions?"

"Sort of," AJ said. "It takes a lot out of her to respond. She only has a little bit of energy every day. When she does something big, she won't appear for a few days, as if she needs to build up her strength again."

"What has she done big recently?" Roland said, fascinated.

It surprised AJ that Roland believed her, believed in ghosts. He gave ghost tours. Did he actually believe in his subject? Know that some ghosts were real?

Then again, he'd been to the inn and seen Gladys knock pictures off the wall in the office.

"She sent me a vision," AJ admitted.

"Really?" Roland said. His excitement multiplied. "What was it of?"

AJ described the books, bound by a leather strap, as well as the cloverleaf.

"You might want to check with some of the antique dealers in town, see if they have any books or straps in their inventory, or remember seeing something like that," Roland said.

"That's a really good idea," AJ said. She hadn't even considered that.

"I'd start with Lee's Antiquities," Roland said. "Caitlin would be your best bet. Then maybe try Treasures by the Shore, though Sally's inventory leans into more kitschy than antique."

"Thank you," AJ said. At least she now had some idea of what to do with that clue.

"As for the cloverleaf, the Byrnes were Irish. So were a lot of the original settlers in Milltown," he said. "It could have something to do with her family."

"Do you think she might have been hinting that it was a family member who killed her?" AJ mused.

Roland shrugged. "I have no idea. You're the psychic. You tell me."

AJ merely shook her head, laughing softly. "I'm so new to this."

"What, you didn't have powers making you crazy when you were a teenage?" Roland teased.

"Well, sort of," AJ hedged. She remembered when she'd told Bea about her visions, and Bea had reminded her of the times when she'd done those sorts of things regularly. However, she'd been so intent on being "normal" that she'd stepped away from her gift, not used her powers.

"I really didn't start having visions until May of this year," AJ admitted. "Just before I came down here."

Roland nodded, encouraging her to continue.

AJ paused. Though her gut told her that she could trust Roland, she wasn't certain. After all, he'd been so angry with Phoebe Reed, when she'd come into the historical society. Maybe he was just trying to find out what she knew, to hide his tracks better.

"But there's another mystery to solve, that's more recent," AJ said. "Phoebe Reed."

Roland grimaced. "Yeah. Her."

His entire attitude turned cold. AJ could almost feel the arctic wind blowing from him.

Phoebe really hadn't been his favorite person.

"Turns out she was a bookkeeper, as well as a bookseller," AJ said.

Roland paused for a moment. "Huh. I'd forgotten about that. She was, wasn't she?"

His hesitation gave AJ pause.

Roland had known all along that Phoebe was a bookkeeper.

He just didn't want to talk about it.

Too bad.

"I take it you didn't use her services?" AJ asked.

"She didn't do personal taxes. She only worked with businesses," Roland said. "The bigger ones."

AJ's eyes grew wide. *That* was why no one she'd spoken to used Phoebe's services! She only worked with the businesses in town, not individuals.

"Mrs. Reed made a presentation to the board of the historical society, soliciting our business," Roland continued, his voice hard. "One of our members does our taxes for free, but Phoebe claimed she could find extra deductions for us, that would more than offset her fees."

AJ could tell that wasn't the entire truth. Roland was lying about something. But what? Which part?

"Why did the board choose not to work with her?" AJ said.

Roland frowned and shook his head. "She wasn't the easiest woman to work with. Her fees were pretty extravagant. Plus, the 'deductions' she found were of questionable legality, at least according to a third-party accountant who did us a favor, looking over her paperwork. According to him, she was applying tax law creatively, and the board's pretty conservative."

AJ nodded, very appreciative of his insights, while at the same time, uncertain of how much of what he'd just told her was the truth and how much of it were lies.

However, she was certain, given what she'd just learned of Phoebe's "creative" use of tax law, that it was a client of hers who'd killed her. A business client.

But who?

Chapter Ten

Lee's Antiquities, like many of the businesses on the coast, took their "weekend" on Monday and Tuesday, so they could be open on Saturday and Sunday, when tourists swarmed the town. The other shop that Roland had mentioned, Treasures by the Shore, was only open Friday, Saturday, and Sunday.

AJ had cut back her hours at the inn as the staff grew more confident in their ability to handle issues, gradually working her way out of a job, and only worked Wednesday mornings instead of all day. Right after she finished that Wednesday, she headed down Main Street to Lee's Antiquities. The day was surprisingly nice, with blue sky and the sun shining thinly down, warming her hair. Thick rain clouds lay on the horizon. Probably come sunset they'd be in for another downpour. AJ was of course dressed appropriately in layers, in a rich, silky, purple blouse, a gray vest, and gray slacks—the ensemble somewhere between office chic and just comfortable. She carried her raincoat, in case the rain decided to arrive early. Her shoes were sensible, black flats that had enough cushioning that she could stay on her feet all day.

The antique shop was located in one of the old, original buildings first erected when the town was created. It was named McCoy's and built in 1915, according to the building marque hanging just below the roof. The walls were made from a dark-red quarried stone that had been left unfinished, so it had a rough, pocked looked to it.

However, that was the only thing about the building that wasn't polished. All the stores had beautiful window displays, the roof was made from scalloped wooden shingles painted a warm gray, and the trim matched. These were AJ's colors, no matter what Bea said about it being too somber. They certainly made this place look sophisticated.

The building started at the corner and took up half a block. A high-end children's toy shop was the first store, with colorful Halloween displays filling the large windows. After that was a small investment firm, the gold lettering on the windows and leather furniture inside telling AJ that she couldn't possibly afford their fees. The antique store was at the end of the building, just before the narrow alley.

Lee's Antiquities hadn't bothered with the Halloween theme that everyone else appeared to have indulged in. Then again, their clientele probably wasn't seasonal. They had a large online presence, which was how the brick-and-mortar shop survived.

The door was recessed between two large display windows. The window on the left featured the sorts of things one might find in an old-fashioned children's room, like an antique crib, a tiny bed with a brass bedframe, and a wooden high-chair. It also had creepy dolls and toys lining the walls and sitting in a row in front of the window.

The other side was a kitchen, complete with huge butcherblock in the center, a weird looking cabinet full of torture instruments, and lots of knives.

Okay, so maybe they did have a Halloween theme going on. It was a lot more subtle than the fake cobwebs, spiders, pumpkins, and witches' hats most of the shop windows displayed.

AJ remembered meeting Caitlin Lee at one or two of the chamber of commerce meetings. She was a pleasant woman who'd left her job in Seattle to come back to Milltown to take care of her parents and their business when they'd gotten ill, then never left after they'd died. She was a little older than AJ, probably in her mid-fifties, happily married, with no kids. Her husband worked remotely, some sort of computer gig.

The interior of the shop was brightly lit with overhead florescent lights that were better suited for a cubical farm. They certainly didn't flatter the hulking pieces of furniture made out of dark wood strewn across the wooden floor. The air smelled of lemony furniture polish, and felt surprisingly dry. A humming sound led AJ to the answer for that —a huge industrial dehumidifier took up the entire wall behind the desk, sucking out all the moisture.

Caitlin was helping an older couple, tourists who'd wandered in that afternoon, who were looking at one of the larger wardrobes. It was at least six feet tall, about three foot across and only a couple deep, made from a light pine, with a set of doors on the top, a second set on the bottom, and drawers in the middle. A swirling pattern of holes decorated both sets of doors, elevating its rustic appearance. It wasn't AJ's style, but it still looked nice enough.

AJ had never heard of a pie safe before today, and eavesdropped on the conversation, learning that women used to bake all their pies and other goods on a single day, then leave them in the pie safe to cool. The pattern of holes let air in but kept flies out.

The couple put a deposit down on the piece, the amount making AJ blanch. She didn't have any true antiques in her house, and wasn't likely to get any, not at those prices.

Finally, the couple was on their way and Caitlin came over to see if AJ needed any help. She was a stout woman who looked as rugged as the ox plow hanging from the far wall. If the animal died, she'd just strap herself in and continue working. Her brown hair was cut short but still curled on the ends, as if trying to compensate for the heaviness of the rest of Caitlin's body. Red tinged her cheeks, as if from a constant wind. She was nicer dressed than AJ would have expected, wearing a shiny red, white, and pink checkered blouse and black slacks. Then again, with the prices here in the shop, she probably had to dress better so customers would be more at home.

"Hi Caitlin," AJ said. "I'm AJ. We've met before, at one of the chamber of commerce meetings."

"I thought you looked familiar," Caitlin said. "You work at the inn, right? And you just opened a psychic business? In Ursula's house?"

"That's right," AJ said. She was already used to everyone calling where she lived Ursula's. She figured it wouldn't become known as hers for fifty years or more, or until after she died, whichever came first. "I have kind of an odd question for you."

Caitlin nodded. "You'd be surprised at the sorts of things I get asked. Are you wondering if any of the pieces of furniture in the store are haunted?"

"That actually wasn't my question," AJ said, her brow growing furrowed. "Do you have haunted pieces of furniture?"

The inn had Gladys, so why not?

"Of course we do!" Caitlin said. She gave AJ a grin. "That cupboard over there? The white one? Its doors open and then slam themselves shut when no one's near them."

AJ glanced at the piece of furniture. It was shorter than the pie safe, maybe only five feet tall, with two doors on the top, an opening in the center with a marble counter for serving food, then two more doors underneath. It had been painted white then distressed, so gray streaks of the wood underneath shone through.

Was there anything magical about it? Haunted? AJ had no idea. It didn't glow or look abnormal. It looked like an ugly, beaten up piece of furniture, something she'd pay someone to haul away from her house.

"For a while, we had a player piano that kept turning itself on. Got rid of that one in a hurry," Caitlin said. "And a couple of those dolls in the window? I would swear their eyes follow me when I walk by."

"Oh," AJ said. She wasn't sure what else she should say.

"The next time I have a piece of furniture that's giving me a lot of grief, I'll just call you," Caitlin said.

"Uhm, sure," AJ said, not certain she wanted to get involved with haunted furniture. She still handed Caitlin her card, so she'd have her number.

"Anyway," Caitlin said after she'd tucked AJ's card next to the very modern register on the back counter. "You said you had a question."

Since Caitlin appeared to believe in hauntings, AJ said, "Do you know about Gladys? The ghost at the inn?"

Caitlin nodded. "Sure. Everyone knows about her. Not everyone believes in her, necessarily, but we've all heard the stories."

"Something that appears important to her is a collection of three books, strapped together with a leather strap," AJ said. "You wouldn't happen to have something like that in your inventory, would you?"

"Hmmm. You mean like this?" Caitlin said, turning away and walking toward the front of the shop.

AJ's heart leaped in her chest. Did Caitlin have Gladys's books? Since she had haunted furniture?

However, the pile of books that Caitlin returned with weren't the books from AJ's vision. They were all the same shape, for one thing, four ponderous tomes that looked like law books, with leather bars in bas relief across the back and fancy gold lettering.

The strap looked similar, though the leather color was lighter, and AJ could tell that it was newer and fancier.

"That's the general idea, yes," AJ said. "But the books and the strap were different."

"Oh, that's too bad," Caitlin said. "I had a feeling about these books, which is why I left them in the window. Are you certain?" She shoved them across the counter toward AJ. "You should touch them," she insisted.

AJ reached out and put a hand on the top book, just to see if she could sense anything. All she felt was a layer of dust under her fingertips. The smell of the old books caught in her throat, making her wrinkle her nose to stave off a sneeze.

"Nothing," AJ said. "Sorry."

"I'll keep an eye out for authentic old books contained in a strap," Caitlin said.

AJ gave her a description of the three books, as well as the strap and the buckle, which had seemed to her to be more like a belt buckle, with holes and a tongue, rather than a strap buckle that merely tightened.

"Got it," Caitlin said, though she hadn't taken any notes. She paused, looking off into the distance. "You know, I would swear I've seen books like that before. Not in my inventory. But somewhere else. Maybe I had my own vision. Or it came to me in a dream."

AJ just shrugged. Was Caitlin like Willow, someone who wanted desperately to be magical and yet didn't have an ounce of power?

"Thank you for your time," AJ said as the front door tinkled announcing another customer.

"I'll give you a call later," Caitlin assured AJ.

Or maybe more like threatened.

AJ sighed as she walked back out into the surprisingly nice day. She was still going to visit the other shop this weekend, though she didn't have high hopes about finding what she was looking for.

And she still had no idea what the four-leaf clover was all about.

Maybe next time Gladys came to see her, the ghost would be able to answer more questions.

Chapter Eleven

AJ HAD a busy afternoon that Wednesday, packed full of readings. She'd barely made it home in time for the first one. That had sort of been on purpose. She knew herself well enough to realize if she'd been home, all she would have been doing would be worrying.

It wasn't the same as doing the short three-card reading. This time, she had forty-five minutes with each client and did a full spread of the cards, letting them ask questions and going into more details. The words just flowed from her, the pictures and symbols on the cards pointing the way.

Her clients appeared to appreciate what she had to say and the readings went reasonably well.

Until the last one of the day. AJ had given herself fifteen minutes in between clients, just to clear her head and to give herself something of a breather.

However, the last client had just barged in after the previous client left, instead of waiting in the entranceway for AJ to fetch him. He was a large man, and for a moment, AJ thought she was confronting Warren Truman's brother.

He had that same shaved head, iron gray hair, and cold eyes that would have looked good on a drill sergeant. However, the triple chin and extra hundred-plus pounds the man carried meant he wouldn't have survived a single day of bootcamp. He wore a scruffy T-shirt with a faded beer logo on it, though his jeans were clean and possibly new.

"I'm here for my reading," the man sneered.

"All right," AJ said, still gathering up the cards from the previous client. "Just give me a moment."

"What, so you can look me up on the internet?" the man said. "Tell me all about myself from my social media accounts? No."

"I don't do that," AJ said. "Why would I? I'm not here to try to trick you."

"Sure," the man said. "Just tell me all the pretty, vague lies that sound like they're the truth when really they don't mean a damned thing."

AJ looked at him, confused. "Why do you want a reading if you're not going to believe anything I say?"

"Because," the man said, crossing his arms over his chest, refusing to say anything more.

What, was this some sort of non-believer who was here to discredit her? Ursula had warned her of people like that, who sometimes made appointments. She hadn't been bothered by many of them, as she rarely had complaints about her services.

"All right," AJ said as she shuffled the cards. She normally insisted on getting payment before a reading. Ursula had set that up as a policy and AJ had followed it. Sometimes, people didn't like paying for her services, but going through the credit card company to recoup their losses wasn't easy, and Ursula made a point of always fighting such shenanigans.

"Please, sit," AJ said.

"I suppose you want me to tell you why I'm here," the man said as he slumped down into the chair.

"No, actually, I don't," AJ said. "I want you to think about your life, about your situation. Think about the question you want the cards to answer. Don't tell me."

"Okay," the man said, obviously taken back by AJ's insistence.

The cards felt stiff in AJ's hands. She had had this issues a couple of times. Normally, the cards felt warm and pliant.

Right away, she knew that she was going to have difficulty seeing anything. She was going to be pulling hard to get symbols out of the cards, to make any sense of what they said.

If it had been for any other client, possibly a regular, once AJ got established, she might be able to call a halt to the reading and have the person come in some other day.

She knew she couldn't do that with this asshole.

"This is you, the querent," AJ said as she laid down the first card.

At least it looked appropriate. Nine of staves. Eight of the staves formed a wall behind a young, wounded man holding the ninth, looking warily over his shoulder.

"This crosses you," AJ said, laying the page of swords across the first card. Swell. More vigilance and spying.

AJ continued the reading. Almost all of the cards were about a bad past and nothing good in the future, either.

The last card—what the querent had to look forward to

—nearly made her laugh. Ace of cups, reversed. The house of the false heart.

She tried to string something coherent to say about the man's question. There were just so many false trails, though, so many unresolved questions. Nothing was as it seemed.

AJ ended with, "Whatever path it is that you're currently seeking, it isn't going to bring you joy. Not with all the secrets you have hiding."

The man sat there and stewed for a moment. "That's it? That's all you have to say about it? Just vague warnings? Nothing specific?"

"The cards are very specific," AJ said. She pointed to the symbols that warned, again and again, of secrets that would consume him. Of all the falsity in his life. "You're living a lie," she said softly. "No one else knows about it, no one is watching you. Your vigilance has paid off in that. But it keeps you separated. Isolated. You won't actually allow anyone to help you."

While the cards didn't specifically say that he wouldn't move forward until he came out from whatever shell he was hiding behind, that was the definite impression that AJ received.

The man shook his head. "No. You're wrong. I got plenty of friends. I go out a lot. Drinking with them."

"And talking?" AJ asked, tilting her head to the side.

"I don't need to listen to this," the man blustered.

"You are correct. You can leave. Now," AJ said.

She already could feel a headache on the horizon, like the rain that was just about to fall.

"Fine," the man said. He stood up, yanked his wallet

out of his back pocket, then tossed a single dollar onto AJ's table. He turned and stomped out, slamming the front door as he left.

AJ sighed. She was tempted to use tongs to pick the money up off her table. Maybe she should burn it, as part of the cleansing that she was going to have to do to get rid of that man's stench.

"Hello? Is anyone here?" called out a new voice.

AJ sighed and pushed herself back from her table. Someone must have come in. She hadn't taken to locking her front door between sessions, though she'd certainly considered it.

"I'm sorry, I'm closed for the day," AJ said as she walked out into the entranceway.

The expression of the person sitting there went from hopeful to crestfallen. "I see," he said.

He looked like a little mouse of a man, with pale skin, a pointed nose, thin mustache, and beady eyes. His hair was dark brown and fell in greasy hunks over his forehead and onto his collar. He wore a faded blue jacket with a name stitched above the left breast, Elliot. Given the dark stains, AJ assumed he must work as some sort of mechanic. However, his fingernails were clean, so maybe he just liked the jacket. The T-shirt underneath was plain gray and didn't hide the fact that he had no muscle tone. She'd place him in his mid-thirties to early forties.

"I'm actually booked for the rest of this week," AJ said. "But maybe next week?"

The man shook his head, biting his thin lips together as he stood. AJ was five foot ten, and had a good five to six inches on the guy.

"Any chance I could get a reading before then?" he said. "Like maybe tonight? It's really important."

AJ shook her head and regretted it. That headache was coming on strong.

"Sorry, not tonight," she said. "I've been doing readings for clients all afternoon and I don't have anything left. What is this about?"

Normally, AJ never asked her clients about their questions for her. It was much better for her to go in "blind" as it were, and just allow the cards to speak.

There was something off about this guy though.

Possibly. Or maybe not. She might just be sensing left-over residue from the nasty customer before him, as well as the stupid headache that was looming and threatening to burst her skull open.

"I'm Elliot Reed," the man said. "Phoebe Reed's son."

AJ blinked. Dang it! She really, *really* wanted to talk with this man.

She peered at him again. He seemed too old to be Phoebe's son. The woman had only been in her sixties. Then again, if she'd had Elliot when she'd been in her twenties, he could be forty. A hard-lived forty.

"I'm so sorry for your loss," AJ said.

Elliot shrugged. "We weren't close," he warned.

AJ could only imagine. No one, it seemed, had been close to Phoebe Reed.

"I don't raise the dead," AJ warned. "I don't hold seances or things like that. I don't even know if she's a ghost or could be talked with."

"But maybe you could tell me something about her? Like where her books are?"

"Her books?" AJ said, feeling stupid. Phoebe ran a bookstore, right? Wouldn't her books be there?

"She left some debts," Elliot said. "I'd like to get in touch with her clients, see if they owed anything to her. But I can't find her books. Her accounting books. Or her list of clients."

"Huh," was all AJ could think to reply to that.

"I've been all through the house. Through her desk and papers. She stashed them. Someplace safe. I just don't know where, though," Elliot said, sounding frustrated.

"I see," AJ said. "And you'd like for me to find her books?"

"Yes!" Elliot said. "If you think you can."

He sounded a bit challenging with that last part. Though he must have been desperate to turn to a psychic.

AJ opened her mouth then shut it again. Up until then, her clients had asked about their lives, seeking solutions for issues they were having.

No one had asked a very specific question about a very specific thing they needed to find.

"I can try to do a reading," she said. She raised a hand at his hopeful look. "Not tonight. I'm serious about not having anything in me tonight," she added.

"Okay," Elliot said, nodding. "Can I come by tomorrow night?"

"Sure," AJ said, though she suspected that wouldn't be ideal. She was going to need time to recover from what she'd been doing that evening. Plus, she'd have to work all day tomorrow. Would she have enough to help this man?

She was determined to try, particularly for Phoebe

Reed's son. Those books might hold clues about who had killed her.

AJ and Elliot exchanged phone numbers and made arrangements for the following evening. Then she shooed him out the door, taking down the "Open" sign and firmly closing and locking the door. She turned off the neon "Psychic!" sign in the window as well, then took herself back to her kitchen for a late dinner.

She barely ate anything though, as the headache made its force known.

Just as the heavens opened up and released buckets of rain, the pain in her head bloomed, and she took herself off to bed.

Maybe tomorrow would be better.

Maybe, with Elliot's help, she could find Phoebe's killer, and then only be dealing with a cranky ghost.

She could only hope.

Chapter Twelve

THE MORNING DAWNED GRAY, chilly, and damp. AJ didn't feel any better. Pain stretched in a tight band across her forehead. Her eyes felt dry and pinched. The back of her skull throbbed, as if caught in a vise.

She wasn't about to call into work sick, though. There was a tourist group coming down—an association of writers who'd rented out half the inn. They'd booked not just rooms but had negotiated for the café as well, intent on using it as a collective writing space in between meals.

Fortunately, this wasn't their first time at the inn. It appeared to be an annual retreat for them. However, AJ needed to be there to help out at the front desk as people started arriving.

Payne would be cooking some additional meals for them. There were a lot of food allergies in the group, because of course there were. These were all artists. One of AJ's first meetings that morning was with Payne, to make sure that he had everything he needed, as well as to smooth the way.

Eva had warned AJ that Payne didn't react well to change. AJ would say that was an understatement.

She would think that someone working at an inn, with a variety of clients coming in every weekend, would have at least some ability to change.

Resistance, not resilience, appeared to fill Payne, though.

AJ had stopped by the Storm Brew Café on her way into the inn to get whatever concoction Juli (with the little heart dotting the "i" of her nametag) came up with to help. However, Juli wasn't there that morning, with her aggressively cheerful attitude. Instead, it was a stranger to AJ, a young man with the properly surly attitude of a barista.

She settled for a London Fog coffee, but the new guy put too much vanilla syrup in it, making it sickeningly sweet. AJ dumped it out on her way into the inn, knowing that the coffee that Payne made would be far superior, at least that morning.

The writers hadn't started arriving *en masse* yet, so AJ had time to go talk with Payne before hanging out up front.

No one was in the little café off the side of the reception area, so AJ headed back into the kitchen.

"Hello?" she called as she walked into the small but industrial space. It hadn't been modified since the inn had changed hands. Stainless steel counters filled the walls, along with a small walk-in fridge. The sanitizer was running in the corner, probably the last of the morning's dishes. Scents of lemon and detergent took over the air, despite whatever Payne had cooking in the huge pot on the stove.

"We're closed," came the surly reply.

Payne stood at the counter with a huge butcher knife in

his hand, ready to defend his territory. He was still the most handsome individual that AJ had ever seen. Gray kissed the temples of his rich, full, black hair, giving him a distinguished look. Piercing blue-green eyes stared daggers at her, from under a broad, intelligent brow. His thin lips were pursed in a frown, the cleft of his chin jutting out stubbornly. The apron he wore covered most of his plain gray T-shirt but somehow still accentuated his broad chest and muscular arms.

Though AJ had grown to trust Payne a little, he still made her hackles rise. He exuded a fanaticism that she would never respond well to.

She couldn't help but compare him to Roland, who managed thoughtful cuteness mingled in with his rugged handsomeness. However, Roland might still be a killer, and he'd lied to her, so she couldn't think about him, couldn't trust him.

"Good morning to you, too," AJ said, trying to lighten the mood though a part of her just wanted to yell at the man. "Are we meeting this morning?"

"Uhm, yeah, sure," Payne said. He glanced up at the clock above the stove and winced.

Yes, he was already ten minutes late for their meeting that morning.

AJ wasn't about to point out that she was just as late, having only arrived at the inn moments before.

"Can you give me five minutes to finish up back here?" Payne asked, already turning back to his chopping board.

"Sure," AJ said. "I'm going to go get a coffee, then sit down in the restaurant."

"Thanks," Payne said, not looking up from his work, his "art."

AJ didn't think she would mind how fanatical Payne was about cooking if he was any good at it. However, she'd learned early to go over his menu plans before he executed them. Despite his training, he had no idea of how flavors went together.

Or worse, he did know, and was just experimenting and "expanding other people's horizons" with unlikely taste combinations that never worked.

AJ helped herself to the coffee in the air pot that was sitting in the café. Though it was just as bitter as she'd suspected it would be, it was still better than what she'd poured out. A touch of honey and cream made it much more palatable, and she didn't end up spilling any of it down her gray-and-white checkered blouse, so bonus.

Rosita and her sisters, the new owners of the inn, hadn't found the money yet to revamp the café, but it was fairly high up on the list of things that needed improving. Once they decided to move forward, it would be up to AJ to convince Payne to take a vacation for two weeks while they did the work.

The café was a throwback to the 1970s, which had probably been the last time it had been updated. And not in a chic, vintage way. Cheap wood paneling covered the walls as well as made up the booths that lined the edges of the dining area, all of it dim and dingy. Yellowed, scratched resin covered the tops of the tables, protecting the historic photos, postcards, and buttons with old slogans on them that were less-than-artfully scattered across the tops.

AJ took her usual table in the corner, facing the

entrance to the café so she could warn anyone away. The only person who came to see her, though, was Payne, and he wasn't even that late, only eight minutes after she'd seen him in the kitchen.

He hadn't bothered changing, though he'd washed his hands and fetched himself a cup of coffee as well.

"What did you want to see me about?" Payne said as he sat. He managed to not sound surly, just resentful.

"The writer's group is coming in this afternoon," AJ said. "We were going to go over the menus."

Payne started off with a rant about individual meals. AJ let him blow off steam for a bit. She'd learned from Eva that letting him have his head at the start of any encounter made him so much easier to handle afterward.

Eventually, he ran out of steam and got to the point. He'd come up with some good ideas for dealing with the various allergies in the group, including a baked potato bar where people could add their own fixings, with chicken on the side for those who insisted on animal protein.

AJ only had to nix a couple of items—seriously, no one was going to want to put garbanzo beans on their potatoes, though she kept the tofu, because, you know, *writers* and *artists* and who knew what all they'd want?

As Payne seemed content to just sit there for a moment after they'd finished, AJ found the courage to ask about Phoebe Reed.

"While all life is sacred, and I would never advocate harming a living creature," Payne said slowly, "Phoebe Reed *was* a very difficult woman."

"She had a bookkeeping business, in addition to her bookstore," AJ said, prompting him.

Payne nodded. "She took care of some of the bigger businesses in town. Like Riley's Real Estate, and Sally's Seashore Rentals."

AJ felt her eyes grow wide. Those were pretty big firms, based in Milltown but with affiliates up and down the coast.

She would think that Elliot should be able to go to those businesses to get Phoebe's business debts paid. She'd have to remember to tell him later.

Maybe she'd track Fred down as well. He might have a more complete list of Phoebe's clients.

"Who do you think shot her?" AJ couldn't help but ask.

Payne grimaced. "Could have been anyone. The bullet probably came from a Glock, 17. 9mm semi-automatic that are extremely common and what the FBI prefers these days. I see it all the time at the gun club."

AJ nodded. There was an indoor gun range nearby that many of the locals used. Bea, for the short time she and Peter had owned a gun, had also used it.

"Does Roland Jax belong to the gun club?" AJ said. She hadn't meant to ask that question out loud, particularly given the surprised look that Payne gave her.

However, then he slowly nodded. "He does. And he has a 9mm like that. Why? Did you have a vision about him or something?"

"No," AJ said firmly. She wasn't about to cast suspicion on someone unless she knew for certain.

Payne narrowed his eyes at her. "You know something," he accused her.

AJ shrugged. "He certainly seemed to dislike her. Tremendously."

"Well, she tried to screw over the historical society, once," Payne said slowly. "Had volunteered to do their taxes. Though the board hadn't okayed it, someone slipped her the information anyway. Rumor has it, Roland did it, though he denies it. Her interpretation of tax law was *creative* to say the least. Luckily, someone else caught it and they didn't end up sending a questionable tax return into the IRS."

That was *almost* the version that Roland had told her. Except the part where it hadn't been okayed by the board before Phoebe had started doing the taxes.

Had Roland at one point not been so negative about Phoebe? And had she taken advantage of him?

Phoebe had certainly seemed oblivious of his feelings. Then again, since no one seemed to like her, maybe she'd been willfully blind.

"All right, thank you," AJ said. "Do you know anything about Phoebe's son? Elliot?"

Payne looked startled. "I didn't think she had any kids. She wasn't married." He paused, then shook his head. "But she didn't always live here, either. Maybe he's from an early marriage."

"That's what I was thinking," AJ said. "He said he's looking for her accounting books."

Payne snorted. "Yeah, I bet. She probably kept more than one set of books, one to show the IRS and a second that had the real numbers. This Elliot should check her safe."

"What safe?" AJ asked. Why did Payne think Phoebe would have a safe?

"If I was her? I'd have a state of the art safe installed somewhere in her home. Not a usual place like a wall, either." Payne nodded. "And if she was really smart, she'd have hired someone from Seattle or Olympia to install it, as well. That way, you couldn't just call up Bergerman's, the local shop, and ask about it."

"I'll mention that to him," AJ said.

"How did you meet him?" Payne asked.

"He came by for a reading last night, after my last client," AJ said.

"What did you tell him?" Payne said, obviously curious.

"To come back tonight," AJ said with a grimace. "I was just too tired, and the headache that showed up has never backed down."

Payne peered more closely at her. "Huh. You do look pale. Stay here. I have the perfect fix for you."

AJ nearly said no, but Payne had already scooted out of the booth and was heading back toward his kitchen.

She heard him bustling away back there, as well as the bing of the microwave.

He came back out handing her a steaming cup of something that actually smelled good.

"What is it?" AJ asked, cautiously blowing on it.

Payne sighed before he answered. "I can't actually take credit for it. It's Sooli's *da ji ma*."

AJ couldn't help but grin at him. Chicken soup with some special herbs in it, according to the Asian woman who worked at the reception desk.

"I won't tell anyone that you fed me something you

didn't make," AJ promised after taking that first divine sip. The heat appeared to relax her face, something the coffee hadn't done, and she could feel the edges of the headache starting to let go.

Payne shrugged, raising his hands wide. "I do not advocate eating flesh, or taking the life of another. However, there is something to be said about the regenerative powers of chicken soup."

"Thank you," AJ said. Thus fortified, she went back to her office.

Only to walk into what felt like an arctic chill.

Chapter Thirteen

"HELLO, GLADYS," AJ said, happy for the warm cup in her hands.

AJ had put a large, indoor thermometer on the wall, just so she could check Gladys's effects.

The temperature back there registered a mere sixty degrees, despite how warm the thermostat was set.

Fortunately, AJ knew that it was a location-based shift. As soon as Gladys left, the area would warm right back up.

AJ sensed a lot of frustration from the ghost. She'd gone straight into her meeting with Payne instead of walking into the office first, so Gladys had been waiting for her for a while.

"What is it?" AJ asked.

Gladys rattled all the picture frames on the wall in response. No words formed that morning.

Just rage.

"I am trying to find out who killed you," AJ assured the ghost. She told Gladys how she'd gone searching for the stack of books, what she'd learned.

That appeared to mollify Gladys slightly.

"What can you tell me about those books? Why are they important?" AJ said. She'd asked this question before but had never gotten a good answer. All that she ever received was the sense of weight, how heavy those books had felt.

"Your family was Irish," AJ continued. "Is that why the four-leaf clover was important?"

A sigh went through the room, stirring the chilly air and making AJ shiver.

AJ again had the feeling that the ghost did, but didn't, know why she had given AJ the vision that she had.

"Is there anything you can tell me about the books? Or the four-leaf clover? Anything at all?" AJ pestered.

With a final frustrated whine, Gladys swept from the room, rattling everything, even the papers on AJ's desk before she departed.

These sorts of responses were why AJ was more inclined to believe that Gladys was the ghost of the daughter, not the wife, of Oscar Byrne.

When Gladys had first asked her to solve her murder, AJ had gone to Roland to see what was known about the girl. She'd died sometime during the first year the inn had been open, though of what had never been reported. Roland also claimed that there was no obituary, no memorial service.

That happened sometimes, particularly when someone died of something communicable. People didn't want to admit that something bad like that had happened to their family, so they hid it.

AJ spent the rest of the morning dividing her time

between her work in the office and helping out at the front desk. She took an early (for her) lunch at twelve-thirty, hurrying out and heading down to the Storm Brew Café, promising to bring something back to Sooli, who'd just started at noon.

Sooli had given AJ solemn instructions that she was *not* to hurry back, but to eat her own lunch first. AJ had meekly agreed, though she was determined to go back a little early.

Fred was missing again from the café. Had he had an argument with Miguel, the owner? Or was his "muse" visiting him at a different place? AJ didn't have time to track him down, though.

Roland was in line just in front of her. When he'd ordered and turned around, catching a glimpse of her, he said, "I have news for you. Come see me after you get your food."

AJ pasted a smile on her face and assured him that she would, though a part of her was frustrated. She knew he'd lied about Phoebe, and possibly his involvement with her. Though her head was better after Sooli's magical concoction, she still wasn't feeling one hundred percent.

Did she really want to add in a confrontation on top of all of that?

Still, AJ picked up her meal—a light salad with a cheese and pastrami panini—then walked over to where Roland sat in the far room, waiting for her.

"Have you heard anything more from the ghost?" Roland asked eagerly.

AJ couldn't help but roll her eyes at him. "She came to see me this morning," she admitted. "Didn't say anything.

Just seemed as frustrated as I am about how little progress I've made."

"Well, I may have another piece for you," Roland said with a grin. "Oscar Byrne was a timber baron, and had quite a bit of money. However, he wasn't the only one who financed the inn. There was a silent group of investors who called themselves Seamair."

AJ looked blankly at him. She could feel her headache start to threaten again along the edges.

"*Seamair* means clover in Irish," Roland said triumphantly.

"Huh," AJ said, intrigued though she didn't want to be. "Was their symbol the four-leaf clover?"

"I don't know," Roland admitted. "But it might have been. Some of the investment groups of the time were very philanthropic, and so had quite a name for themselves. There were a lot of reports and articles written about them. The Seamair group appeared to primarily finance smaller projects headed up by other Irishmen."

Roland's good humor faded slightly. "I've tried to find out more about the group, but there just isn't much to go on. Except that one of their leaders was eventually hanged for organizing a bank robbery."

"Do you think there's something about the financing of the inn that may have led to Gladys's death?" AJ hazarded. "I still think she was just a girl, not Oscar's wife."

"You can ask her, can't you? Now that you know more?" Roland said.

AJ opened her mouth then shut it again. "Maybe," she said. "I'll try tomorrow." She grimaced. She wasn't looking forward to her next encounter with the ghost, as that made her head hurt even more.

"There's one more oddity," Roland said slowly, "about the financing."

AJ waited while he finished off a bite of his own sandwich before he continued.

"Oscar Byrne is listed as the full owner of the inn, after 1913," Roland said.

"Okay," AJ said, not sure what Roland was getting at. Could he please get to the point? She didn't have a lot of time and her headache was definitely making itself known again.

"Most of the other deals that were done at that time wouldn't list a single individual on the deed," Roland finally said. "However, the other strange thing is that Seamair appeared to have nothing more to do with the inn after it opened."

"Did Oscar pay them back?" AJ asked.

Roland shrugged. "Not sure where he could have gotten the money. The entire inn was built for just over $100,000. Which is the equivalent of over two million today."

"Wow," AJ said. She had no idea. "That's...a lot."

"The marble in the front reception area is all imported from Alaska," Roland said. "Have you seen some of the swanky pictures from when the inn was first opened?"

"I have," AJ said. A lot of them had been reproduced and were in the café, decorating the tables. "The lobby had all this amazing furniture in it. And the floors were covered in Oriental silk rugs."

"I've also seen pictures that show that the large

meeting room on the second floor of the main building of the inn used to be decorated just as fancily," Roland said.

AJ nodded. Many years ago, the single big room on the third floor of the inn had been divided up into clunky bits, either too small or too big to be useful for the current day. The wood floors had been covered with cheap carpet, and the beautiful furniture replaced with generic conference room tables and chairs. As their primary customers were tourists, not businesses, the whole area generally stood empty.

The center room of the meeting rooms did still have a rather nice fireplace mantle in it, with the original blue-green tile decorating the edges of it. However, few groups made use of the meeting rooms, and there had been talk of converting them into guest rooms instead.

As the property was on the historic registry, AJ wasn't sure how much remodeling they could do. Then again, that room had already been subdivided, and was no longer in its original configuration.

Maybe they needed to try attracting more groups, like the writers, who would make use of all of the conference rooms.

"So the clover leaf may be because of the Seamair," AJ said after a couple of minutes.

"Thank you," she added.

Roland gave her a half-smile. "It isn't much. But I figured it might help."

They ate together in silence for a few moments. AJ could tell that Roland had a question for her but wasn't certain how to ask.

"Go on," she said, instead of torturing him as she would Bea. "What is it?"

Roland sighed. "I'm that obvious?"

"Yes," AJ said. "Not quite as bad as my sister, but close."

Roland grinned at that. "I have an older brother and a younger sister," he said. "So I understand being pestered about questions."

AJ nodded. "If it would make you feel better, why don't you ask your question first, then I'll get to ask mine?" Her heart speeded up as she formed the words, and the throbbing in her head stepped up too.

Seemed as though she was going to have this confrontation now.

"Do you think you could get Gladys to talk with me sometime?" Roland asked all in a rush.

AJ snorted at him.

"What? I'm a historian. There's so much she could tell us about!" Roland said. "It's part of why I started researching the ghosts in town. I didn't start off with the idea of a ghost walk tour. I was just looking for a better window into the past."

"Are any of the ghosts on your tour real?" AJ had to ask.

"According to my official spiel, of course they are! All of them!" Roland said with a cheeky grin. "Unofficially? There's really only one, other than Gladys, who's ever made any sort of contact. And she can't speak, not to me or anyone else I've brought through." He paused, then added, "I'm really hoping that at some point, you'll do the ghost walk, or even a private version of it, to see if you can sense any of the supposed ghosts."

AJ nodded, not committing.

"So what was your question?" Roland asked.

AJ made herself take a deep breath in, then let out. "I think you lied to me," she said softly, not meeting his eye. "Before. When you were telling me about Phoebe and the historical society's taxes." Only then did she look up.

Roland's glare grew hard. "Is there a question in there?"

"Did you?" AJ simply said.

Roland deflated all at once. He blew out a breath of air instead of arguing or continuing to lie. "I should have known better than to lie to a psychic." He looked out, across the room, no longer willing to meet her eye.

AJ's heart sank. He *had* lied to her.

"It isn't what you think," Roland said softly. "It's complicated."

AJ wanted to give him a chance. She did. He was cute and smart and he smelled good and he was interested in ghosts, in what she did.

However, he'd broken her trust, before anything else could be started. If anything could be between them.

"Mostly, my lawncare business does all right. I work like a dog during the summer, so I have winters off to do historian things, research, reading, all like that. One summer, I had too many expenses and didn't pay enough attention to what I was spending. It was stupid, I know. Ended up in a real hole. Was going to owe a bunch in taxes. This happened three, four years ago, now." He sighed, sounding frustrated at his younger self.

"So I went to talk with my parents about a short-time loan. Just for the winter, because I knew that come the following spring, I could pay them back. I'll spare you the family drama," he said, his voice turning dry. "Let's just say that the conditions attached to that money were too high."

AJ nodded. She'd never been in that exact situation, but she could understand. She would never ask her mother for money. She'd be too concerned about the contract that her mother would draw up.

"One of the suggestions my father made was to contact Phoebe Reed, see if she could help out with my accounts. Like an idiot, I took his advice." He shook his head.

"I gave Phoebe a chance to look at my books. She set up a depreciation schedule that was pretty aggressive, but it did mean I wouldn't have to worry as much about taxes coming up. And she set up an agreement with the IRS to defer my taxes for a year. So she was useful." He took another deep breath. "But I was still an idiot. I had the historical society's records for a short while. I was supposed to be delivering them to another member. They went missing from my truck."

At his long pause, AJ said gently, "Phoebe?"

"Phoebe," Roland replied grimly. "I'm still not completely certain how she managed to steal them. But she did. I reported them missing—I'm not a complete idiot. It was my fault, and I was going to take responsibility." He shrugged.

"Then, at the next board meeting, Phoebe comes swanning in, with full tax forms already completed, claiming to have found so many additional deductions for our 501c3. She also claimed that I had voluntarily given her all the records, as we'd been working together so closely. She implied a lot of things that weren't true," Roland said. "It's taken me a long time to clear my name with the society. At least they allowed me to stay a member, though I'm no longer on the board."

"I'm sorry," AJ said.

"Another board member went through Phoebe's return and pointed out all the errors she'd made, as well as her questionable interpretation of tax law," Roland said. "In response, Phoebe turned around and made a very large, very public donation to the society." He sighed. "They can't forbid her access to the building, they can't stop her from coming to meetings. At least I was the main person she bothered, always coming in with these historical books that she was willing to donate to us. Some of them were actually worth something."

Roland shook his head again, then looked AJ straight in the eye. "I'm sorry I lied to you. It's an embarrassment, both what she did to me and now you, finding out. I'm really so sorry."

AJ waited for the next part, but Roland seemed to believe he'd said everything he needed to.

"If you want access to Gladys, and maybe to get back on my good side, you need to promise not to lie to me again," AJ said. "Just feeling sorry about what you did isn't good enough. You need to actually learn from your mistake."

Roland slowly nodded. "You're right. I'm sorry. I won't lie to you, not anymore." He gave her that lopsided smile again. "I didn't kill Phoebe Reed, though I had plenty of reasons to," he assured her.

Finally, AJ believed him. "Do you think anyone in the historical society did?"

"I don't believe any of the members killed her," Roland said. He held up his hand so AJ wouldn't jump in. "I've thought about it a lot. Phoebe Reed never tried anything underhanded with the society, even though she had all our accounting information for a while. What she did was wrong, but there were never any repercussions from it. Except for me. She always came in while I was working in the society building, always insisting on spending time with me."

"Did you ask her to stop? Tell her that it wasn't appropriate?" AJ asked, curious.

"I did," Roland said. "It wasn't easy. But she discounted my words and never paid attention to my cold shoulder. She was always trying to get me to call her Phoebe. I never did." Roland gave her a self-satisfied smirk. "But I was also powerless. She was a valued patron, and she was making large donations quarterly. I couldn't just throw her out, no matter how much I wanted to."

"Thank you for telling me the truth," AJ said as she finished off her meal.

Roland gave a heart-felt sigh. "You're welcome. I should have done it in the first place. I just told you the story that I want to be true, blaming everything on Mrs. Reed, instead of taking responsibility for my actions."

AJ grinned at him. "See? Was that so hard?"

Roland rolled his eyes at her. "Yes. Yes it was. It was excruciatingly difficult. So when can I talk to Gladys?"

AJ snorted as she stood up. "Let's see if I can figure out who killed her. She won't talk about anything else until we solve this riddle."

"Do you think she'll stick around? After you solve the mystery of her murder?" Roland said.

"I don't know," AJ said. "I know that in stories, the

ghost leaves. But this has been her home for an awfully long time. We'll see."

"Okay," Roland said. He hesitated, then said, "See you around?"

"Yes," AJ said firmly. "I'll come and talk with you later. Even go on that ghost tour of yours sometime."

"Good," Roland said. He gave her a sadder smile, as if he was only just now realizing the full implications of his lying. How, no matter how cute AJ might think he was, it was going to be a long time before she trusted him.

AJ left the dining room, picking up Sooli's order before exiting the café and heading back to the inn.

She believed Roland, that he hadn't killed Phoebe Reed, though he probably had the most reason to.

So who had killed her? And why?

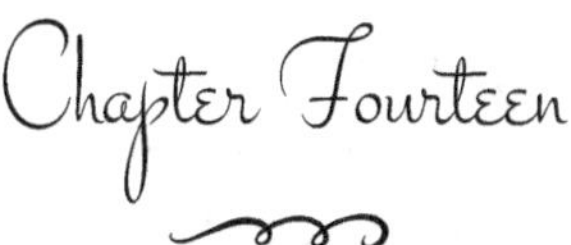

Chapter Fourteen

AJ's HEADACHE never really went away, all through the long afternoon. At least the writers, for the most part, were delightful. They greeted one another cheerfully, were sorry to hear that Irv had passed and Eva had retired, but were happy to meet AJ. More than one of them offered to help *her* that weekend, telling her to let them know if there was anything she needed. Usually, that was her line.

"There's a reason why we always give them a good deal," Sooli said after the most recent encounter.

"I don't get it, but I'm glad," AJ said. It was a change after dealing with some of the more "entitled" guests they'd had that summer.

Payne was still working that evening, having agreed to provide a spaghetti dinner to the group, served on either pasta or spiraled veggie noodles. AJ saw more than one of the female writers walk into the café, only to come walking out a few moments later.

Probably had wanted to go talk with Payne, who'd shooed them away.

Finally, it was time for AJ to go home. She was but wasn't looking forward to it. Being at home would be awesome. Maybe she could finally lie down for a while with a cold bag on her head and break this headache.

Trying a reading that evening was going to be difficult, and likely to cause her more pain.

However, she didn't want to postpone it, or to put Elliot off. She really wanted to solve this murder.

Despite her misgivings, AJ hurried home, made a meal out of the plate of spaghetti she'd snagged from the café, then prepared her reading room.

She was still convinced that doing a reading with the cards wouldn't work. They weren't specific enough.

The thought of having a vision in front of a client made her anxious. She was going to have to ask Ursula about it during their next phone call, which was set up for the next day.

AJ had the impression that Ursula did all of her various foretellings in front of people, reading palms, tarot cards, as well as a type of scrying with her crystal ball. Then again, she'd been working with clients for more than forty years.

AJ filled her scrying bowl with water and set it on the table. She took out some of her beautiful, smooth pebbles and placed them on either side of the bowl so she could grab them easily.

Then she waited. Elliot was late. Had he changed his mind? Should she go ahead and try to have a vision without him?

Eventually, a loud knock came on her door.

"I'm so sorry I'm late," Elliot said, looking flustered. "I

had to drive here from Sunset and there'd been an accident."

AJ could tell that he wasn't telling her the full truth. He probably had driven there from Sunset, but there hadn't been an accident. He'd just left late.

"It's really all right," AJ assured him after he'd apologized for the third time. He seemed so nervous. Was it just because of the reading? Or something else?

There was still something off about him. She was a little more certain of it this time. Then again, it might just be that he'd lied to her about traffic.

"Come into my reading room," AJ said. "I have everything prepared."

They sat at the gorgeous wood table, the sturdy oak feeling steady under her hands.

"So what do I do?" Elliot asked, looking around nervously.

"Just sit there and think about what it is that you seek. Try not to freak out if you see anything. Also, don't disturb me. I'm not sure if you'll see anything in the scrying bowl or not," AJ said. Bea hadn't, this last time she'd had a vision.

AJ took a deep breath, and felt obligated to say, "This is really the first time I've done a reading like this in front of a client."

Elliot seemed surprised by that. "Why is that?"

"I just started, you know?" AJ said. "I'm still learning this business."

Elliot looked horrified. "Wait, you aren't Ursula Krakowsky?"

"No, she retired," AJ said. "She sold me her business and her house."

"I thought I was coming to see a real psychic!" Elliot complained.

AJ stared at him coldly. "I *am* a real psychic I'm just new to this business. Not completely clueless."

Elliot glared at her. "Phoebe Reed swore by Ursula's powers," he said, his words clipped. "That's why I came here. To see *her*, not you."

"Well, I'm who you have," AJ said, trying to contain her anger. It was encouraging the pain in her head, moving it up from behind her eyes and spreading across her forehead. "You can leave now. Or you can stay and I can see if I can solve your problem."

Elliot slowly sat back down. "I'll stay. But you better have something good."

"I'll try," AJ said. "That's all I can promise." She was fairly certain this was a bad idea. Her headache was just getting worse, and trying to have a vision wasn't going to make it any better.

However, now she felt as though she couldn't back out. Elliot didn't believe in her powers. She needed to prove herself.

Earlier, AJ had thought about the chant she'd use for this vision. Though she knew that Payne's advice about a safe was smart, what if Phoebe hadn't had one? It made more sense to merely ask about Phoebe's books and her list of clients.

AJ stared into the water and asked the question, "Where are Phoebe Reed's accounting books? Her books. Her accounting books. Where are Phoebe's books?"

Time slowed and the words became a steady drone in her ears. It felt as though someone else was saying them, while the rest of her was spiraling down into the rising vision. Her body flushed warm, then cold, turning her stomach. The smell of moldy, old books washed over her, tickling the back of her throat. She wished she could pause to clear it, but the vision had her in its claws, talons piercing her skull, making her head throb worse.

Clouds chased across the surface of the water in her scrying bowl. They seemed unsettled, unable to still.

Time dragged on. Sweat drenched AJ, followed immediately by a chill that caused her to shiver. Her stomach protested more strongly. AJ had the sense that this was taking longer than her usual visions. Was that because she was trying to force the issue, as it were? Or was it just taking longer than usual for her magic to find the books?

Finally, the clouds filling the top of her scrying bowl dissolved and she could see the water, which had turned silver, like a mirror.

Slowly, a figure rose up out of the waters. It was recognizable as Phoebe Reed, not so much because AJ could see her face, but because of the ropes of numbers looped around her neck. This time, the numbers were more prominent, solid black against the white and gray of Phoebe's ghost-like shape. They reminded her of *The Matrix* movie with the streams of data raining down.

The vision shifted, like a camera pulling back, showing the room that Phoebe stood in. It looked like an office, with bookshelves across the back wall. The desk had been shoved to the side, the chair knocked askew.

Phoebe floated in midair, her chest raised up, as if her body were trying to fly through the ceiling but the ropes of numbers wrapped around her neck prevented her from escaping.

The numbers flowed out of a spot on the floor. AJ couldn't see a trap door, but she had the feeling that the space there was hollow. The desk had protected it from easy view.

That was where Phoebe's books were located. A hidden compartment.

Phoebe started to fade, the body hollowing out until just the black outline of the shell remained. AJ found her hand moving, lifting the pebbles up to her bowl, about to toss one in and end the vision.

However, the books *behind* Phoebe, on the bookshelf, were now dancing. Where they had space between them, they swayed oddly back and forth, as if blown by winds. Where they were tightly packed together, they slid forward and back, like a silent keyboard.

What, was there a second compartment there? Behind the bookshelf? Or was there something hidden among the books?

On the lower left side, a group of books started glowing.

AJ gasped.

Those were Gladys's collection of books, held together with a strap.

What was Phoebe doing with those? How were the two murders related?

A loud *bang* broke AJ's concentration. It echoed in her ears, like a gunshot. She sat back, dazed. Had it come from the vision? She hadn't seen anyone else.

"What happened?" she asked, her words slurred. She

worked her jaw around and swallowed, her entire throat dry.

"I don't know. You tell me," Elliot sneered. "You were having some sort of fit, staring into the water. You were shaking, eyes big, mouth open. Looked like you were about to start drooling. But I didn't do anything, didn't disturb you, as you asked."

AJ nodded and immediately regretted it. Her headache was worse, so much worse. Ice picks now stabbed her eyes. Her stomach rolled. She was going to be sick. Chills wracked her body, the shivers sending shooting pains down her arms.

"Excuse me," AJ said, pushing herself back from the table.

"What, so you can go do a disappearing trick on me? Not a chance," Elliot said.

It would serve him right if AJ threw up all over him. However, she couldn't bring herself to do that. Not at this point. Instead, she shoved herself from the table and tottered over to the wastebasket in the corner. Her lovely dinner came back up, followed by yellow bile, sour and harsh against her throat.

When AJ finished, she took the stinking can out of her reading room, walking directly into her kitchen so she could stick her head under the faucet in the sink. The cold water shocked her system, but in a good way. It grounded her, bringing her all the way back from her vision, into the present.

The headache retreated slightly. AJ had a touch of vertigo as she straightened up, wrapping her towel around her head.

She turned to go back to the reading room, only to find that Elliot had followed her into the kitchen.

"Sorry about that," AJ said, indicating the trashcan that she still needed to empty.

Elliot peered closely at her. "You aren't faking that, being sick, that's for certain," he said slowly.

"No, I'm not," AJ said. "That reading took a lot out of me."

"What did you see?" Elliot asked. He finally seemed curious and not challenging her for once.

"I think I saw where Phoebe kept her books. In a hidden compartment. In an office," AJ said. "With a lot of bookshelves across the back."

Elliot nodded. "That could be either her office at her house or her office at the bookshop." He paused, expectant. "What else can you tell me?"

AJ felt a strange reluctance to share more details with him. "Visions have symbols in them, like tarot cards. It becomes a matter of interpreting them."

"Then let's go look," Elliot said.

"Not tonight," AJ said firmly. "Not unless you want me to be sick all over you this time."

Elliot grimaced. "You're sure you saw where she kept her books?"

"Yes," AJ said. "I believe I have a clue now." She wasn't completely lying. The books could be in that compartment beneath her desk. But there was something hidden in the bookcase in that office as well.

"And you can't tell me?" Elliot said.

"I think going there would be the best," AJ said firmly.

Elliot blew out a breath and glared at her, obviously frustrated.

AJ didn't blame him. She was frustrated as well, betrayed by her body. She felt as though she was tantalizingly close to solving both murders.

The thought brought her no joy, not with how her head was pounding. She was afraid that if she bent over, her skull would split open and spill her brains out all over the floor.

"Will you be better tomorrow?" Elliot asked.

AJ took a shallow breath and released it, as a deep one would have been too much effort. "No," she said. "I'm sorry. I have to work, then I have clients to see. I could do Saturday, though."

Elliot slid his hands into his pocket and looked away from her, his jaw clenched.

What, was he considering forcing the issue? AJ wasn't kidding. She'd throw up all over him if he tried.

Plus, she was standing next to the sink. There was water there. And more, well, *liquid*, in the stinking trashcan beside her.

If he came at her, she'd be more than happy to use her magic and that water to slap him silly.

"Fine," he said after a few moments. "I can wait until Saturday. But don't try to put me off any more."

"I won't," AJ said. "I want to solve this as much as you do."

She had some clients on Saturday, so she and Elliot agreed to get back together Saturday evening. Elliot would meet her at Phoebe's bookstore, to check the office there. If that turned out to not be the place, they'd go up to Phoebe's house.

AJ was grateful that he would be driving, and that she could just walk to Reed's Reads. She still hadn't bought a car yet. It had been on her list of things to do that weekend. Maybe she could still go car shopping Sunday afternoon...

In the meanwhile, she strongly suggested that Elliot leave. AJ needed to go lie down.

After he left, AJ cleaned out the yucky trashcan because leaving it until the morning was even grosser than cleaning it up now, despite her headache.

As quickly as she could, AJ went to bed with a blissfully cold pillow across her forehead and eyes. It wasn't going to touch the pain in her head, not for a while. The pillow might grow warm before it had done its job. Luckily, AJ had a second one in her freezer, ready to use up its coldness as well.

Despite how awful she felt, she couldn't help but think about the vision she'd just had. Why did Phoebe have Gladys's books? How were the two murders related? Was there a secret compartment under her desk? Or was it behind the bookshelf?

And what had been that loud bang, that had broken AJ out of the vision?

She would swear it hadn't come from the vision itself, but from Elliot. However, he hadn't made the sound, had he? Shouted at her? Something? He'd claimed he hadn't disturbed her, despite how she'd been behaving.

There was another mystery there, but her poor aching head wasn't in any sort of shape to solve it at this point.

Chapter Fifteen

AJ FELT JUST as bad the next morning. She would swear that her head would split open if she moved it wrong. Even putting on her cutest gray-and-red striped blouse with nice gray slacks didn't cheer her up. Her face looked pale, and dark lines marred the skin under her eyes. It took a lot more makeup than usual to make herself at least vaguely presentable that day.

After she finished upstairs, AJ dragged herself down to the kitchen. Normally, she had a hearty bowl of steel-cut oats that she added liberal amounts of frozen fruit to, along with a good dollop of vanilla protein powder. That morning, all of it turned her stomach. Despite nothing being in her system, she could only force down a couple of spoonfuls.

Not even coffee sounded appetizing.

However, it was Friday, one of the busier days at the inn. She was going to work the front desk for part of the morning as well as most of the afternoon. She'd been assured that normally, by the second weekend in October, the inn wouldn't have that many guests. The large group of writers had really made a difference.

Generally, AJ only worked every other weekend. However, because of starting her psychic business, she'd been able to schedule most of her weekends off for the month of October. Come November, she'd work every weekend, as well as over Thanksgiving.

This Friday, she would also take a longer lunch, so that she could stay later that evening if needed. Unfortunately, she couldn't sleep her entire lunch break. Instead, she had a call with Ursula scheduled.

Could she put off her talk with her mentor?

Despite how much her head hurt, her instincts told her no, she shouldn't.

Crap.

Could she cancel her appointments for the evening? Even though she'd told Elliot she was busy?

She'd have to think about that.

The day outside was cold and blustery, gray clouds chasing each other across the sky, hiding the cheery light of the sun. The tide was on its way out, the edge of the water in the mid-distance. The waves looked sullen as they pushed themselves along, lapping at the shore, as if resenting being pulled back. Seagulls whirled overhead, their caws sounding mournful, embodying the old tales of carrying dead sailors' souls.

AJ turned from the water and trudged into town. Going up the shallow incline to Main Street made her head pound more. Black dots danced in front of her eyes. It sounded like the ocean had taken up residence in her head when a sudden whooshing noise filled her ears. She flushed and then had chills again.

Maybe she'd come down with something?

AJ still stubbornly marched on, making her way slowly to the inn.

Willow took one look at her and shook her head. "Goddess! You look terrible!"

"Thanks," AJ said dryly. She'd thought she'd done a better job of hiding her pain.

"Your aura is all skewed," Willow went on. "It's like you're only half in your body."

That...actually made sense to AJ. The vertigo that kept returning made it feel as if her head were floating like a balloon and only lightly attached to her body.

Ursula had told her that Willow had no power. But her reading of AJ had certainly been accurate. Maybe her mentor had been wrong about the other woman.

"Should you be working today?" Willow asked.

"I can push through," AJ assured her.

"Of course you can," Willow said gently. "Nobody would doubt that. But should you?"

AJ had no answer for that. Instead, she said, "Let me go put my things in the office and I'll come back up to help."

Of course, Gladys was waiting for AJ in the office, angry and frustrated as ever.

"Good morning, Gladys," AJ said as she walked into the nearly freezing air. Gladys was certainly making her presence known that morning. The temperature back there was fifty-nine. There was even the vague outline of the ghost standing in the corner, as if she were looking out the window at the garden.

The pictures rattled in response.

AJ held up her hand. "I think I saw your books in a vision last night."

The air grew still, expectant. The ghost-like shape filled in, growing more distinct.

"What do you know about Phoebe Reed? Are you familiar with her at all?" AJ asked.

No words came from the ghost. All AJ could sense was additional frustration. Her visual form faded.

"I take it that's a no, then," AJ said. She paused. There was something else that she needed to ask about. It took her a few moments to dredge it out of her tired brain.

"The four-leaf clover. Was that to do with the investment group, the Seamair?" she asked.

The air in the room changed. If anything, it appeared to grow colder.

With an abrupt gust that left AJ shivering, the presence of Gladys disappeared.

What was that all about? AJ didn't understand if Gladys had responded in the negative or the affirmative to her question. Had Gladys been angry? Scared? Upset?

Dang it! None of this was making sense. Or maybe it was and she was just so out of it she couldn't put the clues together.

AJ sighed, then took herself off to the front desk. She'd considered stopping by the kitchen to see if Payne had any more of Sooli's magical chicken soup. However, the café was still full of guests—probably the writers—eating breakfast, and she knew better than to disturb him while he was working.

Willow was busy with a guest as AJ slid in behind the

desk. Fortunately, another guest came up to check in almost immediately, and the rest of the morning went fairly quickly.

AJ walked slowly back to her house when it was time for her lunch break. It wasn't just because she was exhausted. The cool air felt marvelous, the wind easing the pain in her aching skull. She just made it home in time to answer the call from Ursula.

"Good morning!" AJ said, determined to be cheerful.

"Good afternoon!" Ursula replied, as it was later where she was, in Georgia. "Tell me how you're doing, how everything is going. I heard that your first readings went well!"

AJ grinned and told Ursula about everything, how the readings had gone on Saturday and Sunday.

She made sure to ask about Agnes. Ursula assured AJ that she could afford the readings she'd scheduled, as well as quite a bit more. Seemed Agnes actually *owned* Maureen's Seafood Shack, down on the beach.

AJ rambled on, also telling her mentor about the full readings she did on Wednesday.

"I see," Ursula said slowly. "So you did hours of reading on the weekend, followed by more hours on Wednesday?"

"I did," AJ said.

"So how bad is your headache right now?" Ursula said, exasperated.

"How did you know?" AJ asked, not wanting to admit that she was already contemplating how she could stay on the phone with one of her cold pillows draped across her forehead.

Ursula sighed. "You can't do so many readings in a row.

I might be able to do that now, but not when I'd started. You absolutely shouldn't be."

"I don't understand," AJ said. She tried not to whine. Really.

"Think of using your power like a muscle," Ursula said. "You wouldn't spend the entire winter sitting on the couch like a slug, then get up and run a marathon. Not without hurting something fierce. But that's what you've just done."

"Oh!" AJ said, suddenly understanding. "Okay. So how do I get rid of the headache?"

"Rest," Ursula said firmly. "Don't do any more readings. Not for at least a week."

"I have clients tonight. And tomorrow," AJ said.

"Cancel them. They'll understand, or at least the ones who used to come and see me," Ursula said.

"All right," AJ said, not bothering to hide her grumble.

"It's really for the best, dear," Ursula assured her. "You must rest that head of yours. Let your powers recover. Or you might do yourself permanent damage."

AJ sighed. She really didn't want to let down her clients, particularly since she was just starting her business. Didn't want to ruin her reputation before she'd even begun.

However, she also had to admit that a part of her was relieved at the thought of not having to push herself that evening, to allowing herself some rest.

AJ brought up the client who'd been so disbelieving of her talents.

Ursula told her to never feel bad about not doing a reading. She gave a chuckle. "Those non-believers will never believe. Even if you told them a winning lottery ticket number, that they went and purchased, and then won millions. Their view of the world is set. Though it does sound as though you gave him good advice."

AJ shrugged. She'd done her best. She'd have to take Ursula's words into consideration.

"So what about Phoebe Reed?" Ursula asked. "Have you had any visions about her?"

"I did, actually," AJ said. She wasn't surprised that Ursula knew about Phoebe's death. Though the older woman wasn't that comfortable with modern technology, she'd still managed to install the Milltown app on her phone so she could keep up with all the local gossip.

AJ told her all about her initial vision, as well as the second one, that she'd had the previous night for Elliot Reed.

Ursula paused. "I knew Phoebe Reed. She came to see me, maybe once or twice a year, every year. She was always looking for that lottery ticket, that one deal that would put her on rich row." She sighed. "I didn't know she had a son."

AJ blinked. This was the second person who hadn't heard about Elliot Reed. "Maybe they'd had a falling out? He didn't seem too fond of her. Then again, he's also really frustrated because he can't find her books."

"Don't try to have another vision about those," Ursula warned.

"I won't," AJ said. "Trust me. This headache is going to be really efficient at stopping me."

"Good," Ursula said. "But you shouldn't start pushing the first day you feel better. You need to take the time to fully recover."

AJ bit back her initial response—*Yes, Mom.* Instead, she said, "I have one more question. Last night was the first time I'd ever tried having a vision in front of a client, using my scrying bowl. Did you do that?"

"That was very brave of you," Ursula said. "I would think it took a lot longer than normal, right?"

"It did," AJ said. She didn't nod her head because it was still pounding too hard.

"I wouldn't do it on a regular basis," Ursula warned her. "It takes too much energy to block out the other person's aura. You'd be better to do that sort of reading in private. Ask the person to wait in the hallway or something."

That answer brought AJ a lot more relief. She hadn't been looking forward to having to do that sort of thing on a regular basis.

"One more thing," AJ said. "That reading ended with a loud bang, like the sound of a gunshot. But I didn't see anyone in the vision. And Elliot swears he didn't do anything, hadn't made a sound."

"Phoebe was shot, correct?" Ursula said slowly. "Was she shot in her office?"

"Uhm, no, her body was found in the parking lot of her bookstore," AJ said.

"Maybe you were getting an echo from the past. Maybe there isn't a hidden compartment under her desk. Maybe she was shot in her office and moved."

"That's a possibility," AJ said. Though she'd been following the case like everyone else, the police hadn't released those details.

Then they talked about AJ's initial vision, from Gladys, looking into the past. AJ had thought that Ursula would be pleased with her breakthrough, but her mentor just sounded frustrated with her. "Another vision? Your poor head must be killing you."

"It is pretty bad," AJ finally admitted.

"All right then. You don't need to keep talking to a little old lady. You go rest. Now," Ursula said. "And no readings for at least a week. Possibly two weeks."

AJ wanted to protest. She had been working so hard to build a client list, to start her business off right. Now, she was canceling all those people she'd brought in.

And if Ursula was right, she shouldn't just slot them in wherever. She was going to have to go easier on herself.

It wasn't a lesson she'd ever bothered to learn. Or had to learn, despite how burned out she'd been after leaving her company in Seattle.

AJ didn't know how not to push. That was how she'd gotten along her entire life.

"I'll rest. I will," she finally told Ursula. "I am going to sign off so I can go lie down."

"Do I need to call you on Monday? Check up on you, and make sure you're resting?" Ursula said. "Because I'll fly out there and sit on you if I have to."

"No, Mom, I'll rest," AJ promised, laughing. Though honestly, her mother rarely nagged her that way.

"That's good, dear. I will talk with you next week though," Ursula said. "Instead of in two weeks."

"All right," AJ said. She knew better than to try to argue with Ursula. She'd make it work.

"Next Friday?" Ursula said.

"Yes, I'll talk with you next Friday. Same time," AJ assured her.

After she'd hung up, and gone to lie down, AJ tried not

to feel guilty about having to cancel her clients that weekend. Fortunately, she was connected to all of them via email or text, so she wasn't going to have to actually call anyone.

She set an alarm for herself and willed the cold pillow on her forehead to do its work, to ease the pain in her head. She was going to be fairly useless until she got better.

She hated feeling this helpless, this weak. She also suspected that Ursula was right. She'd been pushing her powers too hard.

As she drifted off, AJ found her thoughts drifting toward that bang that had ended her vision the night before. Had that been a loud warning from her powers that she was at her limit? Was it an echo of the shot that had killed Phoebe? Or was there something else to it, something that involved Elliot?

Her tired brain kept trying to make connections but sleep claimed her before she got too frustrated.

Chapter Sixteen

THOUGH AJ FELT bad about clearing out the next week and a half of readings, a part of her breathed a sigh of relief when she'd finished.

So much for participating in most of the "Witch-tober" festivities the rest of the businesses were putting on. She would be available again before Halloween, so maybe it would be okay.

Hopefully, she hadn't just permanently damaged her business and her reputation.

AJ let herself sleep in on Saturday. Though she went to sleep with a headache, and woke up with one, it finally felt as if the pain was receding. She didn't feel well enough to don her wetsuit and go out for a swim. She still took a long walk on the beach, the cool winds blowing away some of the cobwebs that had gathered between her ears. Despite the chilliness of the water, she did take off her shoes and let the waters lap at her toes, feeling it ground her.

The day stayed clear, white clouds playfully chasing

each other across the expanse of pale blue sky. Gulls and terns raced past AJ as she walked, playing their own games of hide-and-seek with their morning meal. Waves pushed high onto the sand, the tide all the way in, the water greeting her and lightening her mood.

After lunch, and another nap, AJ finally started to feel vaguely human. She was actually considering going and doing her grocery shopping when she got a text.

Mess me?

AJ snorted and shook her head. Bea always spoke her text messages into her phone, then never went back to correct the spelling.

Sure. We'll go with that. Wanna chat?

The phone rang and AJ happily answered.

"So tell me all about your visions!" Bea enthused.

AJ couldn't help but roll her eyes. She still did as Bea asked, telling her about Elliot Reed and the most recent vision she'd had of Phoebe Reed.

"So you think the two cases might be connected? Gladys and Phoebe?" Bea asked.

"I'm not sure," AJ said. "I mean, I swear those were Gladys's books. But she didn't know Phoebe. So I have no idea."

There was a thread between the two murders. But AJ didn't know what it could be.

"You're going to look at Phoebe's office tonight?" Bea asked.

"Yeah, with Elliot. I think that will be okay," AJ said. "I'm not planning on having another vision. I'm just hoping that what I saw will tell me where her books might be."

"I think it's strange that she only did accounting for bigger firms," Bea said.

"I don't," AJ said. "Businesses specialize. Which I wouldn't expect an *artist* to know." She pronounced it as *ar-teest*, as a way to tease her sister.

"I'll have you know that I'm not just a successful *ar-teest*, I'm also a savvy business woman," Bea huffed.

"Uh huh. Sure," AJ said. "And who does your taxes every year? And advises you on all your business matters? And makes sure the pair of you don't end up living on the street?"

"That's just Peter's way of showing me he cares about me, of staying involved in my art," Bea said. "You know. Being a real partner. You should try it sometime."

AJ opened her mouth for a sharp retort, then sighed and forced herself to relax. "Maybe someday I will," she said softly.

"You must still have quite a headache if you aren't going to fight with me," Bea commented.

"You also told me to stay open to the possibility of other people helping me," AJ said.

"What, you're taking my advice? Who are you and what have you done with my older sister?"

AJ just laughed. It felt good, and though the motion jostled her head, it also lifted some of the pain.

"So Peter and I will be down the weekend before Halloween," Bea said. "Do you want to schedule a whole bunch of readings again for that weekend? So I can be there to help?"

"No," AJ said. "I don't think that's wise. Maybe at the start of next year's tourist season. I have arranged to take most of Halloween, that Wednesday, off from the inn. I've had a lot of requests for readings that day."

"The stars will all be aligned and it will be a most fortuitous time," Bea said in a stuffy, officious voice.

AJ rolled her eyes. "That too. Plus, it's supposed to be the time when the veils between this world and the spirit world are the thinnest."

"Ohhh, are you planning on doing a séance?" Bea asked eagerly. "I might drive back down if you're going to try something like that."

"Hadn't planned on it, no," AJ said. "Besides, how does that even work?"

She couldn't see bringing a large group of clients into her reading room, having them all sit around her table, holding hands, the lights dim as AJ tried to call some ghost to them.

Maybe there were people who could do that sort of thing. But AJ dealt with the water. Maybe if the victim had drowned...

"Think about it," Bea said. "It might be fun. And it would bring in a lot of clients."

AJ sighed. "I'm not about to try to bring in clients with claims of powers I don't have."

"But you've just started to figure out what you *can* do," Bea pointed out. "I remember you telling me about the blood thing. It wasn't something Ursula had ever investigated."

"True," AJ said. She'd been trying to figure out more uses for her water witch powers. She'd always been a "hard stick" when it came to any sort of blood draw. She'd been donating blood every month since learning about her powers, trying to accelerate the flow of blood, then stop it as soon as the needle was withdrawn. So far, she'd had mixed success.

She'd never practiced on anyone else. However, if she ever accidentally cut herself, she now felt certain that she'd be able to stop the blood flow. Not that she ever wanted to find out what would happen if she had a major accident.

And a gunshot, well, that would overpower her, she was certain. Even with what magic she had, she didn't have enough to protect herself from that sort of damage.

"So think about doing a séance on Halloween," Bea said. "While I may only be an *ar-teest*, I have been successful at marketing and selling my paintings in Milltown for a while, now."

"You're selling an object," AJ pointed out. "I'm selling an experience."

"True, but I still think a lot of the same marketing techniques apply. Like being friendly with all the other businesses down there. You want them to think of you anytime they hear that one of their customers is having problems," Bea said.

"That's...actually good advice," AJ said.

"Still think you're a pod person when you say that kind of thing," Bea said.

AJ sighed. "I doubt I'll ever be as popular as you are, here." Bea knew practically everyone in town. Eventually, AJ had figured out that was actually part of her sister's marketing plan. She was friendly so people would think of her, would recommend her paintings to tourists, hand-sell them even.

AJ seriously needed to consider doing the same thing, so that people would recommend her services.

"I'll be friendly," AJ promised. "More friendly," she added. She knew that her sister always thought of her being as sullen as a barista in a particularly good coffee shop.

Despite the recent headaches, AJ had found herself, well, happier here in Milltown than she'd been in Seattle. And she'd *loved* Seattle.

Huh. Who knew that under that city slicker exterior lay the heart of a small town girl?

The sisters chatted for a while longer. Bea was disappointed that AJ would be working all through Thanksgiving weekend, but promised to come down and make her a fabulous meal earlier in the week, so she'd have the appropriate leftovers—turkey and all the fixings—to snack on.

AJ just shook head but agreed. Bea was, when it came down to it, a better cook than she was. Or rather, Bea had taken the time to learn how to cook, and while AJ liked to eat, she didn't consider it worth the hassle.

Eventually, they said their goodbyes. AJ promised to text Bea after going to Phoebe Reed's office with Elliot, if not that night then the next morning.

She didn't know if she'd be able to solve the case that night or not.

There was something about the gunshot that still bothered her. When she went into her reading room, it was as if echoes of it still rang off the walls.

It hadn't come from the vision she'd been having. She would bet on that.

But where had it come from? And why?

Chapter Seventeen

R EED'S R EADS was at the other end of Main Street from where AJ lived, almost two miles away. So she left her house an hour before she was supposed to meet Elliot and slowly started walking there.

The moon was in its last quarter, hanging low across the water. The clouds had all scattered, leaving the evening sky clear. Cold winds blew with force. AJ suspected that another storm was coming.

She considered walking down to the bookshop on the beach instead of on the street. However, the moon wasn't that bright and she didn't fancy spending the rest of the evening with sand in her shoes. Maybe on the next full moon she'd take a long stroll on the beach. Except that it was likely to be raining. The fall had been somewhat dry so far. It was only a matter of time until storms gathered daily.

More people were out and about than AJ had expected, particularly given how late in the season it was. Cars continued to drive by on the street as well. She'd read an article about how people were dissatisfied with spending so much money on things and were instead looking for experiences. That might explain why the inn had been so busy, even at the start of the off-season.

Up ahead, AJ saw a group of people gathered on the sidewalk. She considered crossing the street to avoid them, but then she heard Roland's voice.

It was the infamous ghost tour.

AJ walked up to where they stood, gathered on the sidewalk, listening to Roland tell the tale of the McCarthy building and the washing woman who had been found, hung by her own laundry, on the top floor, which had been the servants' quarters.

"Ever since then, when the moon is full, a white, ghostly shape can often be found wandering that top floor, weeping and moaning softly," Roland said. "And here is the town's psychic, AJ Steward!" he said, surprising her.

"Hi," AJ said, awkwardly waving.

She could already hear Bea's commentary about being a dork.

"Can you confirm that there are ghosts in Milltown?" Roland said.

"I certainly can," AJ said. "I've even spoken to the ghost in the inn."

"There you have it!" Roland said gleefully. "Yet another witness to the spooky denizens of Milltown. Are you here to join the tour?" he asked, sounding eager.

"No, I'm afraid I have a different haunting to deal with tonight," AJ said. Which was actually the truth. "Maybe next time."

"I look forward to it," Roland told her with a big grin.

"Now, group, onto the surprising twists that occurred while building Portman Place."

AJ smile and walked away as Roland shuffled his charges along, going in the opposite direction from her. He still had some of her business cards, which she knew he'd hand out to the people who were on his tour.

Unfortunately, she didn't have any slots available for the next week or so. Pretty much any of the tourists who might be interested in her services would either have to be staying in Milltown for a few weeks, or would hopefully remember her when they came back. If they came back.

She'd have to remember to keep a few slots open, just for Roland's tourists. Though the last ghost walk for the year would happen on the weekend before Halloween, when the entire town would have a large celebration.

AJ considered Roland as she continued her walk down the street. She'd told Bea that she wasn't interested in another entanglement, not yet. Her heart was still bruised from Ken and his cheating ways.

At some point, though, she actually did want a partner. Someone who supported her, like Peter did Bea. Not financially, but emotionally.

Huh. She'd never thought about having a relationship like that. Before, she'd always insisted that her partners be as independent as she was, with their own hobbies and interests.

Maybe she'd been going about this whole dating thing wrong, looking for the wrong things. She certainly hadn't found Mr. Right that way. Perhaps she needed to be more entangled with her next partner, though that brought its own fears and boobytraps.

AJ slowed down as she got to the McCoy building. The children's store on the corner had all its lights on, displaying the gaudy spiderwebs and the huge, purple and black spider who crouched on a soft pillow in the corner. The investment place had all the lights off, but the golden letters on the window still reflected what little light there was.

Lee's Antiquities hadn't bothered with any lights in its display windows either. AJ would swear, though, that items in the displays had been moved around. She didn't recall seeing the large block of knives close to the edge of the glass before.

Was that blood, or some other dark liquid, coating the handle of one of the knives?

Then, in the children's room window, AJ would swear that those creepy dolls and toys hadn't been sitting along the edges of the window, but further back. Caitlin had said that she felt the eyes of some of the dolls following her when she walked by.

AJ shivered as she felt the same thing, telling herself that no, that one doll's head hadn't moved as she'd walked by, tracking her.

It was all in her imagination. Really.

Was it possible that the antique store didn't have haunted items, but a playful ghost? One who moved their merchandise around regularly?

Someday, AJ would have to go back to the shop and see what she could feel.

During broad daylight and when she wasn't alone.

The next block held one of the two big grocery stores in town. There were actually three stores that sold food, if she counted the little hippy co-op up on the hill that sold organic foods, as well as a lot of thing in bulk. The two large stores were managed by Fred.

That reminded her that she hadn't seen Fred in quite a few days, now. Was he writing at a different coffee shop? Or, heaven forbid, was he actually working? She was certain that the Milltown app would have reported if something bad had happened to him. Or even something good.

Hopefully, the next time she went to the Storm Brew Café, he'd be in his usual spot, ensconced in the corner and thinking about writing.

Finally, AJ got to Reed's Reads. Lights flooded the parking lot, while the building itself was dark. She assumed that was to keep tourists from parking there, close to the beach, even after business hours. A single car was parked next to the door, Elliot, she assumed.

Though the building hadn't impressed AJ when she'd seen it during the day, it seemed even more decrepit at night, shadows hiding the orangish stucco, the red tile on the roof appearing black. Walking across the parking lot, she noticed that it, too, was in worse shape than she'd first thought, with enough cracks filled with moss that it almost looked like paved bricks instead of a solid surface, though the spacing was uneven.

AJ tried the door, but it was locked. She knocked loudly, saying, "Elliot? It's me. AJ."

After a few moments Elliot opened the door. He looked more weasel-like than mousey that evening. Though maybe that was wrong too, and he just had a rodent furtiveness around him.

As AJ walked past him, she thought she caught a whiff

of something acrid, like sulfur but set further down in her throat.

Her mind immediately went back to that gunshot she'd heard when doing her reading.

Was that gun powder she was smelling? Had Elliot been shooting a gun that afternoon? There was a gun range in town. She wasn't sure how easy or difficult it was to get a membership. She seemed to recall there was a waiting list for using it.

Maybe Phoebe had had a membership and he'd just helped himself to it.

Books loomed on the shelves in the main room, the bookcases tilting slightly toward each other. A stiff breeze and they'd both be buried in books. The smell of the mold made AJ crinkle her noise to hold back a sneeze. She didn't want to step beyond the entranceway, feeling claustrophobic just by the sight of the place.

"How are you?" AJ asked Elliot as she motioned him to lead the way to Phoebe's office.

"Holding up," Elliot said.

It was a perfectly appropriate thing for the son of the murdered woman to say, even if they hadn't been close.

AJ couldn't help but feel that it was a lie. Elliot wasn't holding up, wasn't in mourning for his mother.

No, she'd judge that he was feeling both afraid as well as anxious. Not even eager, not that night.

Something else was bothering him, far beyond the search they were about to conduct.

AJ wished suddenly that she'd brought her big purse, with the water bottle in it. Not that she necessarily could use that water for anything impressive. Still, she noted where the bathroom was, in case she needed to make a run for it and get herself to a ready supply of water.

Phoebe's office was at the back of the building, behind the staging area for the shop. Tattered boxes were piled up beside a work counter, a label machine lying mournfully alone in the center of it. At least it didn't reek so much of old books back here. Maybe because the floor was polished concrete instead of the indoor-outdoor carpet stuffed under the bookcases out front.

Elliot fiddled with keys, trying a couple before opening up the door to the office. It swung outward.

He opened the door wide and gestured for AJ to go inside.

Was this it? Was this the site of her vision?

AJ took a deep breath, released it, then, with her head high, walked into the dim space.

Here went nothing.

Chapter Eighteen

AJ STEPPED into a room that she'd never seen before.

Except, there were echoes of that other room in here. The bookcases all along the walls. This time, AJ noticed that they were full of antique books with worn leather spines, nothing fresh or new. A couple of large filing cases held court in the corner, the locks busted and their contents rifled through.

There wasn't anything special about the desk itself. It looked like a modern computer desk, with a cheap laminate top and drawers on the sides. A small rug sat underneath the desk, where someone would place their feet. A fancy office chair lounged on the other side of the desk, modern black mesh that didn't fit the décor of the rest of the room, which was definitely garage-sale eclectic. Probably the chair was also used.

AJ took her time walking around the desk, then peering underneath it. She even went so far as to touch the carpet.

Eww. Sand covered her palm.

But she didn't get the sense of a space hidden there.

"I'm sorry," AJ said as she stood up. "This isn't the place I saw in my vision."

Elliot stood there with his hands in his jacket pocket. "All right," he said slowly, nodding. "Didn't think this would be. But we had to check, make certain, you know?"

"I do," AJ said, nodding.

"Let's go to her house, then," Elliot said. He turned to go.

AJ paused for a moment, looking at the books behind the desk. She didn't think there was anything hidden there among them. They weren't calling to her, glowing, or giving off any sort of magical clue.

Phoebe had surrounded herself with books, everywhere she went. They were her life. Both as a bookseller and a bookkeeper.

Books also held the mystery of her death. AJ was certain of it.

Elliot had probably already looked at all of these books. They had the feeling of being disheveled, as if someone had taken every single book off the shelf, flipped through it, then slammed it back in place, disgusted and not being careful.

AJ turned to look back at Elliot, waiting impatiently for her at the door. He'd gone through this room. He must have great faith in her, if he thought she might be able to help him locate Phoebe's safe.

Elliot didn't bother locking the office door when they left. Maybe he'd only kept it locked because he thought there might be something valuable in there.

After they exited the building, AJ asked, "I know that Phoebe wasn't from here. Where did you grow up?"

Elliot gave her a wry grin. "Portland. And other places." He nodded. "That big bookstore in Portland? What's the one, that takes up a couple of blocks downtown?"

"Powell's," AJ supplied. She wasn't a big bookstore person herself, but everyone had heard of Powell's books.

"Yeah, that's the one. Phoebe got her start in the bookselling business there. When I was a kid," he added hastily.

AJ just shook her head. He was lying again, though not about all of it. That was the problem with Elliot. He appeared to mix lies with truth all the time, easily sliding from one to the other.

"Had you been to your mother's house before?" AJ said.

"Visited regularly," Elliot said.

That was...the truth, actually.

So Elliot had had some contact with his mother. Strange that no one in town seemed to know that she'd had a son.

They drove up to Phoebe's house. It was up on one of the hills surrounding the town, like most of the houses. However, it was closer to the center of town, in a small, rundown neighborhood. Even though it was night, the streetlights were enough to show more than one house with cars up on blocks in the front yards, weeds taking over what remained. There was even a burned out hulk of a house, stark, scraggly timbers pointing toward the sky like skeletal fingers.

This hadn't been the type of neighborhood that AJ had expected at all. Phoebe was supposedly better off than the rest of them, doing so well with her business.

Or had the neighborhood fallen down around her, and she'd just never moved away to someplace better?

The neighborhood ended in a cul-de-sac, which didn't surprise AJ. That appeared to be the most popular method of building the neighborhoods above Milltown, running a street until the construction workers ran into a densely wooded area, or yet another creek, then capping the street off.

Except that Elliot didn't pull up to one of the houses. Instead, he took a dark driveway that she'd originally missed, rough and covered in gravel. Trees edged close to the road, hemming them in and stealing all the light. Elliot turned his high beams on, though the driveway appeared to be fairly straight.

After a distance—possibly as much as a quarter mile—the road opened up again and they pulled into a clearing, with a house and a garage on the far side.

AJ would have never known this house was back here. The driveway looked like an old service road. Had Phoebe kept it that way to keep away visitors? Maybe. Though AJ hadn't seen them, she would bet that there had been at least half a dozen "No Trespassing" signs posted along the road.

A single light shone from the dark house. When AJ stepped from the car, the evening seemed hushed and expectant. Winds blew through the trees surrounding them. The sky was still clear, still cold, with just a light scattering of stars across it, like a frozen picture. Wet mulch and pine scents filled the air, more wild than AJ had expected. She'd pictured Phoebe Reed as a city creature, more urban than farmhouse.

Maybe she'd been wrong.

Then again, no one had even known she'd had a son.

Seemed that Phoebe had kept much hidden during her lifetime, and those secrets had followed her into death.

The house was a single-story rambler, like most of the houses that AJ had seen in Milltown. However, once inside, she finally saw the opulence that everyone assumed of Phoebe. The floor was covered in beautiful brown-marble tiles, shot through with gold. A rich cream-colored paint took up the walls. Shelves filled with what AJ assumed were expensive collectibles lined the vestibule, like fancy glass and an array of silver serving dishes.

AJ wasn't an expert on antiques, but she'd bet that the little table in front of her was at least one hundred years old, along with the stool beside it. The air smelled of disinfectant, though the pretty bowl full of lavender potpourri was doing its best to overcome it. It was chilly in here, as if the heat had been turned off with Phoebe's death.

Doors opened up on either side of the small entranceway. Elliot turned to the right and opened one. "This way," Elliot said.

AJ hesitated. "Is there a restroom that I can use?" She actually didn't need it. She just really, *really* wanted to run some water over her hands.

"Sure, just past the office," Elliot said.

"Thank you," AJ said. She hurried past him, toward the door he'd indicated. The hallway barely registered—just a long corridor, with beaded light wood wainscoting running three feet tall on either side, and a line of black-and-white artistic photos at eye level.

The bathroom followed that modern design, with bronze tile on the floor, slate-gray paint on the walls, and contrasting white fixtures. More art hung in here, watercolors of stormy ocean scenes, all grays and blacks with just the slightest hint of blue. That blue was picked up with the towels hanging next to the sink and stacked in the shelves next to the tub.

It looked like a magazine spread, not some place anyone used regularly. Was it the guest bathroom? Must be. No woman, particularly not a woman who'd worn as much makeup as Phoebe Reed, used this room.

Fortunately, not only did the bathroom have a toilet and sink but also a standing bathtub with clawed feet. AJ rapped her knuckles on the side, ascertaining that it was, indeed, made out of cast iron.

That assured her more than she could say. She didn't know why.

She flushed the toilet in case Elliot was listening, then ran water over her hands in the sink, letting it pour down from the standing faucet and into the bowl. Then she splashed water onto her face, wishing she could stick her entire head under the faucet.

When the water started to take on a slight glow, AJ resolutely turned her face away.

Though she'd been feeling better since she'd stopped trying to use her powers, she wasn't about to force the issue now. Particularly not with Elliot waiting for her in the other room.

With regret, AJ turned off the water, dried her hands and her face with the fluffy towel next to the sink, then went out to face whatever was coming next, despite the sense of dread overtaking her.

Chapter Nineteen

THIS TIME, AJ stepped into a room that was familiar. Not because she'd been there before, but because this was the place of her most recent vision. The only difference was that the big wooden desk was in its proper place instead of being closer to the middle of the room.

Bookcases lined the walls behind the desk, like poor sentries overlooking the owner's work. Lamps stood in the corners, with decorative glass bowls. The ceiling rose up, far above her head, giving the room an airy feeling.

And there was a pile of books on one of the lower shelves on the left-hand side, held together with a strap. Gladys's books?

Looking at the room in person, AJ saw a lot more details. The overhead light glared down harshly on the scene. She'd bet that normally, Phoebe lit the place with the black torchiers in the corners. Heat suffused the room, unlike the vestibule, as if the temperature had been turned up quite a few degrees to keep its occupants uncomfortable and sweating. Windows lined one wall, dark eyes staring blindly out into the night. The floor was covered in expensive laminate planks, designed to look like natural hardwood and doing a good job at it.

The air held an acrid smell, that same gunpowder scent that AJ had smelled earlier. Plus, the scent of disinfectant was stronger here. Underneath all of that lay a coppery scent.

Phoebe hadn't been killed here, had she been? Her body had been found in the parking lot of her store. Had it been dumped there? If she'd been killed here, it might have been a week or more before someone found the body. If not longer.

Elliot was looking at AJ expectantly.

"Well?" he asked.

"This is the place I saw," AJ said, nodding. She forced herself to take a step forward into the room, then to keep walking across the floor.

Yes, she was there to find Phoebe's books.

However, she was now certain that those books on the shelf were Gladys's books. She felt drawn to them, as though they contained an irresistible magnet. She placed one hand on the stack. Cold raced up her arm, as if she'd placed it in a freezer.

Or as though she'd been touched by a ghost.

"We've never talked compensation," AJ said slowly, turning toward Elliot.

He shifted from one foot to the other. "I want you to find Phoebe's books. Then we'll talk payment."

AJ nodded. "I want these books for payment," she told him as she patted the stack. "Nothing more."

"Why? What do those books contain?" Elliot asked suspiciously.

"Nothing related to Phoebe Reed's death," AJ assured him. "You can look through them. They're antiques that belong to the inn."

Elliot looked confused, but AJ wasn't about to explain further.

Instead, she walked over to the desk. "Here. Help me move this out of the way."

"You think the safe is under the desk?" Elliot asked. "I didn't think to check the floor there. That would be a pain in the ass to get to."

"True," AJ said. "Which makes it a good hiding place."

The pair of them lifted the desk and got it pushed to one side, slanted almost exactly how AJ had seen it. Then she rolled up the rug, exposing more of the laminate floor.

Close up, she didn't see any seams in the flooring.

This was the spot, though. She was certain of it.

After a few minutes of futile searching, AJ stood up and walked back toward the door, trying to find her original vantage point.

There. She hadn't been looking for the compartment far enough away from the wall. The spot hadn't been directly under the desk, where one would put one's feet, but a little forward of that.

For a moment, the square blazed with a bright light, outlining its location.

AJ glanced at Elliot, but he hadn't seen anything. He was still looking in their original location, where the desk had been.

AJ walked directly over to the location, telling Elliot, "It's here." She used a finger to trace the barely visible seam.

Elliot gave a low whistle. "You found it."

"I found something," AJ corrected. "We don't know what's under here."

Elliot tried using his fingers to pry up the square, but he couldn't get any leverage.

"How do you open it?" he whined.

AJ glanced at the desk. Was there a remote control hidden in its drawers?

She found her gaze drifting back toward the bookshelf behind where the desk had been. The books has been shifting in and out in her vision.

"Let me try something," AJ said as she stood back up and walked over to the bookcase.

She closed her eyes for a moment, trying to see exactly what her vision had been telling her.

There. On the second shelf. The book on the end. That was one of the ones that had been prominent in her vision.

AJ slid that book out of the case. The book felt heavy in her hands.

A loud click echoed behind her.

Eagerly, AJ turned to see.

Nope. Just unlocked one of the locks on the cover.

She looked back at the bookcase, trying to remember the other books that had slid in and out.

There was a second book on the same shelf as the first one she'd pulled out. As soon as she moved it, another click followed.

The third one was in the second bookcase, down and to her right.

The fourth and final one was up high. Fortunately, AJ was tall enough to reach it. Elliot would have needed a stool.

With a last ominous click, the square in the floor lifted up.

Elliot sat there with his mouth open. "Wow," he said softly. "I never would have found that on my own."

AJ nodded, pleased with herself. She hurried over to see what the hidden compartment contained.

Purple and blue velvet bags sat on the top. AJ recognized them as jeweler bags.

Elliot looked as though he was about to toss them to the side, when AJ took them carefully from him.

The first bag held a beautiful diamond pendent necklace. The center stone was at least a half inch across. The second was a luminous pearl necklace with matching earrings. Probably not worth as much as the diamonds, though AJ would bet that they were still valuable. The third bag contained a delicate diamond-encrusted watch.

"Whose were these? Your grandmother's?" AJ guessed.

"How would I know?" Elliot grumbled as he continued to pull bags and papers out of the safe.

That was strange. Was it because it was all women's jewelry? Surely he'd know something about the pieces.

Elliot pulled up a binder next. AJ recognized the Jax family's name on the spine—probably Phoebe's will. Again, she rescued it from Elliot before he tossed it away carelessly.

At the bottom of the foot-deep compartment lay a large ledger book, with a black cloth cover. It was ten inches high and almost twice that long.

"Yes!" Elliot said, crowing.

AJ smiled and opened the binder she'd rescued, glancing at the first page.

As she'd guessed, it contained the last will and testament of Phoebe Reed.

Her eyes caught on a paragraph midway down the page.

The document stated that Phoebe had no children and no living heirs. Everything was supposed to go to the historical society.

AJ blinked, holding herself very still.

No one had known that Phoebe had a son. Elliot certainly didn't look anything like the dead woman. And come to think of it, more than once he'd called her "Phoebe Reed." Never once had he referred to her as "Mom" or "Mother."

Who was he, and why had he wanted her accounting books so badly?

AJ gulped and looked up.

Straight into the barrel of the gun Elliot pointed at her.

Chapter Twenty

"I REALLY HADN'T WANTED to kill you," Elliot complained. "You seemed like a nice enough lady. And you've helped me out, finding this hidden compartment."

AJ nodded, clenching the binder that held the will tightly in her fingers.

She had to escape this room. Get to the bathroom, or any source of water.

"Why?" AJ said. "Why kill Phoebe? Just to get at that book?"

Elliot sighed. "I hadn't meant to kill her. You gotta believe me. It wasn't premeditated or something like that. I was just so *frustrated* with the old cow."

"What is in that book?" AJ asked, nodding toward the large black journal that Elliot held with his other hand.

"This?" Elliot said, holding it up with a grin. "This contains the *other* books that Phoebe did, the real accounting. Not the fake set of books that she used to convince the IRS that my organization was barely breaking even."

"Your organization?" AJ said. Suddenly, pieces fell together. "Are you part of the Seamair group?"

Elliot looked shocked, then narrowed his eyes. "No one is supposed to know that name. You really are a good psychic," he added, nodding. "Shame to have to kill that talent."

AJ frantically searched for something, anything, to keep Elliot talking.

"Was Phoebe threatening to go public with those numbers?" AJ asked.

"Naw," Elliot said. "We just wanted to find a different bookie. Someone who was easier to work with. Plus, she was getting old and less sharp than she used to be."

Elliot sighed again. "So the bosses sent me to go collect this thing. Came in here, threatened Phoebe. She refused to tell me where it was. Wouldn't go into any details about it. She made me so mad. Blood boiling angry."

"Did you kill her here? In the house?" AJ had to ask.

"See? I knew you were good," Elliot said. "Yeah, I did. Out in the hallway. Hadn't meant to. Gun went off by accident."

"Why did you dump the body in the parking lot of her store?" AJ said.

Stall. She had to stall. Had to distract him. Get him to wave that gun around again.

Sure, there might be another accident. But he wasn't a stone-cold killer. She had a chance. She could get away.

"Bodies are messy," Elliot said seriously. "And they're hard to be around. You ever been near a dead body before?"

AJ shivered, nodding. She remembered Dewey

hunched over in a pile, like discarded laundry, just inside his front door.

"Couldn't work here, not with that body just lying there. So I moved her into the parking lot of her shop. Cops would know that I moved the body. But they didn't make it part of the press release or anything. So I knew I had some time. I had cleaned up this place well enough that they didn't find anything when they went through it the first time. Took me all night."

AJ was impressed at his industry. "Why the store? Why not just out in the woods near here?"

"And bring one of her redneck neighbors out to investigate? No thank you. Those people are crazy," Elliot said. "It was why she stayed here. None of her neighbors would've ever answered any questions about her. Hell, one of them said that it would be a second Ruby Ridge if the cops ever did come knocking on her door." He paused and grinned at her. "And they aren't about to report the sound of a gunshot nearby."

"How did you get her keys?" AJ asked, still stalling, still trying to figure out how to get out of this room alive.

"Took 'em from her, after she went down," Elliot said with a grimace. "Patting down a dead body isn't my favorite thing to do."

The way he said it made AJ realize that he'd done it before. And would probably have to do it again.

"You really don't want to do this," AJ said. She wasn't about to beg, or promise that she wouldn't tell the authorities about him. Not only would she be lying, she'd never been that good at it.

Instead, AJ forced herself to look away from the gun, toward the open door of the office.

"You're right. I don't want to kill you," Elliot said. "But I gotta."

Out of the corner of her eye, AJ could see Elliot's expression grow concerned.

She forced her eyes to grow wide and let her mouth hang open.

Drool wouldn't immediately form and start dripping down, though she considered forcing the issue, in order to sell it.

"What is it?" Elliot snuck a glance over his shoulder then returned his attention to her. "What are you seeing? Are you having another vision?"

Slowly, AJ nodded, though she didn't look at him. "There," she said, her voice a broken whisper.

"Where? Where?" Elliot asked, looking from side to side.

AJ was no expert at fighting. She waited for just a second more, then lashed out with the binder holding the will.

It was a lucky blow. She knew that. It caught Elliot in the temple and he crumpled to the side.

Not knocked out though.

And he still held the gun.

AJ was up in a flash and racing out the door of the office, down the hallway to the bathroom.

She slammed the door and locked it, knowing it wouldn't last long.

Then she hopped into the tub, turning the shower head on.

The water was numbingly cold at first, pounding down on her back as she stayed bent over in the tub.

AJ barely heard the loud thump Elliot made as he shoved his shoulder against the door.

"AJ! Come out! I'll make it quick," he promised.

She just kept her head down, crying out when the first of the gunshots rang through the room as Elliot shot out the lock. She belatedly stuck her fingers in her ears, though those weren't adequate. She was going to be deafened for a while.

The bathtub didn't save her from any of the shots. Being low enough in it did, as a shot rang out over her back and hit the wall beside her. Flecks of white tile rained down.

Finally, the door burst open and Elliot came through.

He smirked when he saw her in the tub, the water finally warming. "Good," he said. "Being in the bathtub will make cleanup so much easier."

AJ held her hand scooped at her side, ready to splash Elliot. She waited as he took one, two steps closer.

"Goodbye," Elliot said. "And thank you for all your help."

Before he could pull the trigger, AJ raised the palmful of water and threw it at Elliot.

Time slowed, like it did every time she'd tried this, forming the water into a shape.

However, icepicks immediately started hammering her temples as she fought to transform the wave into a giant fist.

The splash of water did gain mass and force. A huge wave struck Elliot, hard enough to knock him over. The gun went off again, this time aimed at the ceiling as he fell over.

Almost immediately, Elliot rolled to the side, stretching his fingers out for the gun that he'd dropped.

AJ wasn't out of the woods yet. She stood up and yanked the hand-held shower sprayer down. Then she aimed it directly at Elliot as he rose shaking to his feet.

This time, aided by modern water pressure, AJ's magic was more effective. The blast of water struck Elliot hard in the chest, lifting him off his feet, out the bathroom door, and slamming him into a wall in the hallway.

AJ jumped out of the tub. Dark stars danced across her vision. She wasn't about to be sick again, though if she was, she was absolutely going to throw up on Elliot this time.

She grabbed one of the hand towels from next to the sink and carefully wrapped it around the gun before leaving the bathroom. The water may have erased all of Elliot's fingerprints from it, but she wasn't about to leave it, either.

Elliot appeared to be unconscious, lying on his side at the foot of the wall, his eyes closed.

AJ raced back to Phoebe's office where her purse—and her phone—still were, grabbing the leather-bound collection of books on her way. She dialed 911 as she hurried out of the house, slamming the door behind her.

Dispatch stayed on the line and talked with her while she went to stand at the far end of the driveway. She figured she was less of a less visible target down here, while at the same time, keeping her eye on the front door, in case Elliot came out.

Luckily, the cheery red lights of her rescuers showed up before he did.

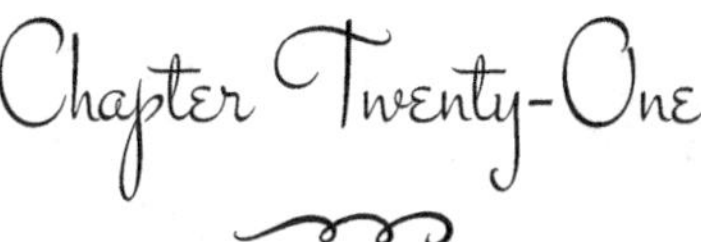

Chapter Twenty-One

AJ SPENT much of Sunday resting, recovering, and trying not to be sick. Her headache had returned with a vengeance, and she found it difficult to do much more than to lie in bed. Bea even threatened to drive down and drag her to a clinic to get her head examined.

AJ promised to go see a doctor if her headache didn't lift in a few days.

She was surprised when someone knocked on her door around one PM. Turned out to be Miguel, from the Storm Brew Café. He wore a stained raincoat with a big floppy hat to protect his head. If she'd passed him by in the street, she would have thought he was a laborer, not the prosperous owner of one of the local cafés.

"Heard you were laid up," he said, handing over a bag that held a bunch of large to-go containers.

"Bea?" AJ guessed, gratefully taking the food. She had some things in her fridge, but didn't have the energy to actually cook anything.

"And others," Miguel said.

"Do you want to come in for a while?" AJ asked, stepping back, though she really wasn't feeling up to visitors.

Miguel stuck his head in, glancing around the entranceway. "Nice," he said, nodding. Then he gave her a grin, looking like everyone's favorite uncle. "You drink some soup, then go back to bed," he instructed her firmly.

"Yes, sir," AJ said. She didn't nod her head. That might bring her more pain.

The soup turned out to be butternut squash, with a drizzle of cream across the top of it and roasted pine nuts sprinkled on it. Comfort food of a sort. AJ ate half of it, saving the other half for later. The other containers held AJ's favorite sandwich (cheese, turkey, and tomatoes in a grilled panini), fruit salad, and a small slice of decadent flourless chocolate-hazelnut cake that the Storm Brew Café didn't serve, but the coffeeshop down the street did.

Touched, AJ took herself back to bed as instructed. Normally, she could never take naps, or even lounge in bed all day, unlike a certain younger sister she could name. However, bed appeared to be the only place she wanted to be for the day.

By Monday morning, AJ felt much recovered. The vague echoes of her headache remained, circling her skull with a light band of pain. However, she felt as though she could stand up and do things and not have her head break in half.

She resolved to work only half a day that day, and take the afternoon off to rest more.

She would have taken the entire day off, but she felt an obligation to Gladys, to show her the books, to finally solve the ghost's mystery as well.

The day was cold and rainy. Winds blew strongly off the water, trying to batter her down, get her to lie down again. A few birds braved the winds. Maybe it was like a workout for them, getting stronger in such weather. AJ faced into the squall for a while, letting the air cleanse her and chase away the last of the fog in her brain.

It was easier than she'd expected to walk up the incline from her house into town, even carrying the books tied together with a strap. She took a detour on her way to the inn, walking up to the Storm Brew Café.

Juli stood behind the counter taking orders, her T-shirt showing off the new ink down her arm. She squeed when AJ handed her a five-dollar bill and told her to make a "whatever."

"I heard what you did, finding Phoebe Reed's killer," Juli said as she added a splash of this syrup, a shake from that canister.

AJ had no idea what she was going to get, but she trusted Juli to make it delicious.

"I still feel stupid, that I didn't realize Elliot wasn't her son," AJ said.

Bea had told her to get over herself, she couldn't know everything. Even if she was a psychic.

"People aren't always what they seem," Juli said seriously.

AJ turned to look at the young woman. She'd always been aggressively cheerful. She sounded solemn for once. And she looked slightly pale.

"Are you okay?" AJ asked, stepping up to the counter.

Juli gave her a watery smile. "Sure! I just need to pick my heart back up again, you know?"

"I do," AJ said. "My ex was a real a-hole."

"I'll be fine," Juli told AJ as she handed over the cup of deliciousness then waited expectantly while AJ took the first sip.

"Chai?" AJ asked. She took a second sip. "But that has a lot of layers in it."

"Yes!" Juli said. "It's a dark espresso chai with coconut milk and just a hint of vanilla powder."

"It's really good," AJ said. The spices warmed her chest, all the way down. She hadn't realized how unsettled she'd been feeling until just then, as the coffee did its job and grounded her further. "Thank you," AJ said. "This is amazing."

Juli just grinned at her. "You're welcome," she said. "Thank you for looking out for our little town."

AJ pondered Juli's words as she walked up the sidewalk to the inn. Bea had harped on this, more than once. That the people in the town of Milltown looked out for one another, took care of each other. That was why Miguel had shown up on her doorstep with food she hadn't ordered, why Roland had been sending her clients.

It was a strange way to live.

But AJ thought she could get used to it.

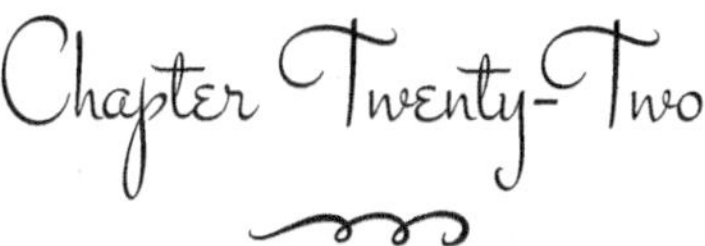# Chapter Twenty-Two

"GOOD MORNING, GLADYS," AJ said as she walked into her office.

It wasn't as cold there as it had been last week. There was a distinct white figure awaiting her in the corner.

"Here," AJ said as she placed the books in the center of her desk. "I found your books."

The figure floated over to the desk, growing more distinct.

Finally, for the first time, AJ could discern a little girl's face, wearing a soft, flowing frock. She smiled with delight at the stack of books, reaching out a more-or-less defined hand, running her fingers across the top.

You touch, came the command from Gladys.

AJ sighed. She wasn't sure that was the smartest thing in the world. Her head was only now starting to recover.

Hopefully, this wouldn't drain her more.

She tentatively reached out and placed her palm on the top of the stack. That icy feeling returned, as if she'd plunged that arm into winter.

Instead of a harsh cold taking over, AJ felt a light tickling across her shoulders and down her other arm, like the first of a delicate snowfall.

She found herself sinking down, into the books, into a hazy vision. She realized with a start that this wasn't an actual vision, that she wasn't using much magic to sustain it. Instead, it was a series of images, flowing from someone else.

Gladys, she assumed.

The little brown-headed girl held a four-leaf clover in one hand. AJ could sense her excitement. She planned on showing her papa the first lucky cloverleaf of the year.

The books she carried over her shoulder were heavy, but she didn't mind too much. She held them in one hand as she burst into the office of the inn—in this same room.

Papa was there, sitting at his desk, pen in hand. Two other men were there as well.

It looked as though Papa was about to sign something important. He had his fancy pen out.

Slowly, the image resolved.

The man closest to Papa had a gun out. Held to Papa's head.

He turned slowly, oh so slowly, toward Gladys and the interruption.

Had he meant to shoot? Or had it been an accident?

Pain blossomed in Gladys's chest.

The books grew heavy. Oh so heavy. They dragged her down to the floor.

The last thing poor little Gladys remembered was her papa calling her name.

Then there was just cold and a forgetting and nothing ever the same.

Slowly, the vision receded. AJ's head felt only marginally worse for it.

"Those men were probably part of the Seamair," AJ told Gladys, who still stood in the office, her hands folded in front of her, her head bowed. "They're a shadowy investment group. Still operating, I guess, even today."

She'd learn later that Elliot had turned state's evidence, and was squealing loudly, indicting all of his bosses.

"I'm sorry," AJ added. "I think your death was an accident."

The ghostly figure standing on the other side of the desk started to fade.

Thank you, she said.

Then she was gone.

Chapter Twenty-Three

AJ DIDN'T RUN into Fred for three more days, back at the Storm Brew Café. However, instead of taking notes occasionally in a notebook and spending the rest of the time looking out on the street (and gossiping) he was actually typing furiously on a laptop.

He stopped and gestured her closer as soon as he saw her poke her head into the room.

"AJ!" he said gleefully. "So good to see you! My muse!"

"Uhm, what?" AJ said. Her head was definitely improving, but she wasn't back to one hundred percent. Had her still somewhat foggy brain missed something?

"I've been working on My Book for so long," Fred told her. "And I still am," he hurried to assure her.

"Okay?" AJ said, unsure what he was wanting from her.

"I've never been able to get it exactly right. I've been trying for years, you know," he admitted.

AJ just nodded, letting him continue.

"It finally occurred to me that part of my problem is that I'm just not ready to write The Great American Novel.

Not yet," Fred continued. "I need to get better as a writer. That means starting to write other things. So I'm writing murder mysteries!"

"That's good," AJ said, surprised. "Wait, you're actually writing?"

"Yes!" Fred said, beaming at her. "And it's all due to you! Your example! I've always loved mystery books. So why not write a few? Set in a small town? With a charming psychic and her steadfast sidekick, the town's gossip?"

"So you're writing about me?" AJ said, finally following along.

"With a lot of creative license," Fred assured her. "Nobody would recognize that it's you. I'm already sixty pages in. And I just keep writing! I can't seem to stop! Every time I sit down to eat, or take a shower, or go walk by the beach, I keep getting more ideas!"

"That's good, right?" AJ said.

"It is," Fred said. "Now, if you'll excuse me, I need to finish this scene. But then, I want to talk with you, all about Phoebe Reed and how you solved her case. And how the debonair town gossip helped."

"You got it," AJ said, grinning.

She couldn't help but text Bea, who was as astonished as she was that Fred had actually started writing something.

Who knew? He might actually finish it, which would be a first for him.

AJ would be there to support him, as the town had been there for her.

But hopefully, the rest of Fred's stories would come strictly from his imagination, and not another death in their small town.

Sign up for my newsletter and I'll start you on your travels with a free copy of my book, *The Island Sampler*.

http://www.LeahCutter.com/newsletter/

Leah Cutter tells page-turning, wildly creative stories that always leave you guessing in the middle, but completely satisfied by the end.

She writes mystery of all sorts. Her Lake Hope cozy mysteries have been well received by readers, who just want to curl up and have tea with the main character. Her Halley Brown series, revolving around a private investigator who used to be with the Seattle Police Department, leave you guessing at every turn. And her speculative mysteries, such as the Alvin Goodfellow Case Files—a 1930s PI set on the moon—have garnered great reviews.

She's been published in magazines such as *Alfred Hitchcock's Mystery Magazine* and in anthologies like *Fiction River: Spies*. On top of that, Leah is the editor of the quarterly mystery magazine: *Mystery, Crime, and Mayhem*.

Read more books by Leah Cutter at www.KnottedRoadPress.com.

Follow her blog at www.LeahCutter.com.

Read more mysteries at www.MCM-Magazine.com

Reviews

It's true. Reviews help me sell more books. If you've

enjoyed this story, please consider leaving a review of it on your favorite site.

Come someplace new...

Do you enjoy exploring strange new worlds, new cultures, new people?

Journey into the various lands envisioned by Leah Cutter.

Sign up for my newsletter and I'll start you on your travels with a free copy of my book, *The Island Sampler.*

http://www.LeahCutter.com/newsletter/

Buy More!

Did you know that you can buy directly from the Knotted Road Press website?

https://www.knottedroadpress.com/shop/

* 9 7 8 1 6 4 4 7 0 3 8 4 7 *